the
lonely
ones

MCCLELLAND AND STEWART LIMITED *toronto/montreal*

james
bacque

*t*he *l*onely *o*nes

The Canadian Publishers
McClelland and Stewart Limited
25 Hollinger Road, Toronto 16

PRINTED AND BOUND IN ENGLAND BY
HAZELL WATSON AND VINEY LTD
AYLESBURY, BUCKS

contents

And ye shall hear

of wars and rumours of wars:

see that ye be not troubled:

for all these things

must come to pass,

but the end is not yet.

MATTHEW 24:6

to **e**lisabeth

the
lonely
ones

London and Paris

My life is chaos. Home far away, Shirley angry if I do
this, friends thinking me mad. But I am not worried.

Au contraire, I walk through this soft April sunshine
in Hyde Park to think objectively of my situation and of myself,
Harry Summers, blond, turning twenty-eight, slightly thicker
through the middle than I want to be, having sold a number of
first-class paintings to some first-class people for second-class
prices, but never mind, my next rise is in sight, and officially in
love with the darling Shirley where I suddenly lose objectivity
in warm and lolling flesh falling into my eyes my hands my
heart and far away from all this some part of me still has not
crossed the Atlantic ocean to England, to these soft small hills
and short tree-walled distances, these avenues of antiquity
leading not over the earth but gently back through centuries of
experience into a green past which is no longer mine. What is
mine?

What indeed walking over wet grass through the smoking
air which nevertheless cannot yet kill the flowers. Here everything is impossible, I am hemmed in, and yet this was my
abode my place of refuge, the where I could no longer be
reached by the voices of madness, voices of home. I have
changed all the conditions of my life, and now life is changing

me within the conditions, and chaos is the result. My unhappiness should result, and yet all I can accuse myself of is inability to tell Shirley the difficult truth and have it over with. When that is done, all will come clear, I fool myself in thinking, knowing that I fool myself, so that all I am doing is luring myself into doing it at last, for her sake and mine, not believing that all will be Niagara peach blossoms when I am finished, but merely better than it is now.

My predicament is solvable, but I have seen hard situations before, I have just enough edge to know what may happen. First, Shirley's tears, inability to understand, which is why I have been postponing the whole bit. How shall I tell her, when shall I tell her, and how shall I say she can't come with me as well, when I have spent the last years of this my painterly life convincing her that she is the all, the peach blossom of my woodhard heart. It would be nice to go away somewhere by myself again and paint, like that time in Vadheim, like Ronda and Hydra and all the early morning places of my life I have seen. If what I know now, I had known then.

Off your butt, Summers, and get the Morgan and go to Pont Street and all the rich Maddivers to kiss her outreaching cheek covered with the fine blush of my arrival, and then off to that party tonight with Mike. Just do as you have plotted, and in the finest of surroundings, let her have it right in her English softness like a snowball. But Jesus, Harry, not in this mood, this is Shirley you are thinking of, not the end of the world. Soften your look, you grim-lipped bastard walking blond head down through the greyfoggy park. Don't frighten the pigeons. Slow your walk and brighten your cheek and open your eyes and look around, for you will make it all up to her in the end. Who are you trying to kid?

Out of the warm mist you walk into a brightly lighted hall and she is very beautiful standing there waiting for you, and she says "Hello" and you take her in your arms and you kiss her, and she is young and beautiful and soft and happy and life is okay. In fact, great. Hard to believe that you are here in the hall with Shirley and you say and hear your own voice saying something banal like "Good evening, Shirley." Which makes her smile. "Come and look at the loot, Harry."

"Well, Mike's waiting."

"Aren't they super?"

"Super. What are they? I know. A hundred trivets and a' and a'."

"No, look, a double electric blanket from the Mossops. More sterling from the Maclennans. And look what Mike sent." A vase.

"Don't you like it?"

"Yes, if it's paid for. Jolly nice of Mike to do that much though, considering he owes me about ten quid. We must go, dear." And her mothing about the table in the library that only the uneducated such as I would ever from a colonial background call a den.

"Come on Shirl." At the door waiting for her to stop adoring our beautiful future all laid out cold and accumulative about us. Harry and Shirley's future written in silver. Now the shout from upstairs. Elder Maddiver on his way down.

"Look here Harry, I just remembered. You must have these. D'you think they'd fit?" His kindly, just-lost-the-Empire-look handing me fine trousers doubtless Dak's. "You can take them in automatically at the waist."

"Would they be a bit short in the leg?" Him holding them against my shaggy bags probably mail order long ago from Eaton's.

"No, perfect, eh?"

"Yes, they're fine. Hurry Shirl. We must go. Sorry to rush. Bye bye." Mr. Maddiver's smile.

"Say thank you, Harry."

"Yes, of course. Thank you." Waving him off and out the door to the steep steps to Mike in the Morgan.

"He's a good old scout, Shirl. I love him." The old bastard. Round to the driver's seat and laying the pants trousers on Shirl's lap where she keeps them home and safe. Very domes-

11

tic girl this. Settles there as if with babe in lap. Nice. Out for a domestic drive in the suburbs. The old fraud.

"My man could get five quid for these aisy." Mike's chest-oh voice from the dim back of the two-strap unpaid-for blue-fart Morgan.

"And doubtless will if I don't put them in the anti-Mike cupboard."

"Good evening, Shirley, and how has this lad been treating you? Better than his old friend Michael, I hope?"

"Mike, thank you for the vase. It's awfully nice."

"Yes, thank you Mike. Just the thing to put some flowers in."

"Best thing I could find."

"It'll be our very first repossessed wedding present, Shirl."

"Not bloody likely. Put it on your old man's account at Selfridge's, Shirl."

God, this lovely man. "You probably did, you probably did. Mike, you're a treasure. Don't go back."

"I have to Harry. Woodbine's been open for a month and I've been handicapping those nags all my life. Smell of the turf, sound of the hoofbeats, feel of the light-orange brand-new hard-currency hundreds. I wouldn't have stayed so long here if the season weren't so long. But now it's Woodbine and Hialeah and Bluebonnets and Sea Island and all the way to Mexico when it's cold enough to see a mare's fart."

And now Mike broadcasting his race from the back seat:

"It's Shirley's Lad on the rail into the first turn closely followed by Shirley's Mum and Rich Daddy, then Babyface, Wet Diaper, Night Howler, Council Flat, Bankruptcy and far behind is Bachelor Days . . . and now to the Grandstand here at beautiful Woodbine Park in Toronto for the moving ceremony and ritual and glowing pageantry of the awarding of the shillings for this the one-hundredth Running Of The Queen's Nose, here she is ladies and gentlemen, lovely Liz Windsor, in private life the Queen of England, imported specially for this one occasion by the management. Here she is and a big hand for the little lady. Lizoh! 'May husband and Ay aw jolly glad to present you with these gold sovereigns, as a token of victory in this great race.' And now the winner, Mad Daddy Maddiver, owner of Shirley's Lad, accepts the prize from the Queen of Ex-Queens in the brilliant air of this spring afternoon in Tarana as this moving pageant comes to its close and we return you to our studios downtown for Jazz at the Vatican with Paul and the Cardinals. Go Paul." And Mike's fabulous invisible puckerlips trumpet blasts from the back seat into our ears laughing at his Canadian wilderness madness.

Ah, fine, after the London traffic a party and all these fine people awaiting us within. Nowt to do but enjoy ourselves at the door waiting for this friend of Shirley's to welcome us with a blank stare at Michael not knowing he was coming. And "Jesus Mike," going in to doff our coats, "I thought you had been invited," introducing him on the doorstep to our host.

"That's because you have a proper mind, old man. Couldn't conceive me coming without, eh?"

"You're very embarrassing. You're only fit to run a pub."

"With a bit of nicker on the side from the nags, I trust, and unlimited credit to my friends who introduce me at the last moment to all the best places. This dark upstairs room looks fine for a touch of what ails us during the night, eh?" Mike, head on side, moving his eyes so fast around I can't even imitate him. And out the hall with the last blast of his magic trumpet to announce his presence, King of Pomposia. How did I ever go halvers on the bluefart Morgan with this guy about to run out to Canada and send me the rest ho ho.

Down to see if Shirley is back to this seething mass yet. It's only nine o'clock and already the air is blue with smoke. Jack with the red lining and the hunch over there. A wave. Wavering through the little-known room I am looking at nothing but necklines. Little round necklines, big round necklines, pale white high ones resting uneasily on the dresslip like pale wine on the goblet's edge waiting to be tipped up. This one neither high to conceal absence nor low to reveal anything. Familiar and Shirley's.

"How." With the hand up. "I recognized you by your cut-water."

"My what? Did you see that Jack Ross is here?"

"Yes." BBC. *Observer*. And all like that.

"He's doing some kind of survey."

"He has eyes for you." And here he comes flannelling up with his wretched friendliness, lips out for the savouring kiss of my bride. Always suckering onto her like a lamprey. Lucky she has her apples packed away tight tonight. Even this friendly greeting for me, and I am glad to see him, the fraud, red lining and all. Red-brick lining. "How are you Jack? Nice to see you and Shirley again." Oho, that's neat, Harry.

"Hello, Harry. We're doing a survey, Mordecai and I."

"And I'm next to be kissed."

"Not yet. Mordecai, this is Harry Summers from Australia."

"How do you do, Mordecai."

"From Australia? Very pleased, I'm sure. What part?"

"Winnipeg."

"Of course, is that New South . . .?"

"Yes."

And now Jack quick as an eel to Shirl. Those apples are mine to polish, Jack, so don't get too near them in their slight black covering. To the dark room upstairs if not observed by Mike. Arrange different saddling times. Where is he? But Jack questioning Shirley and Mordecai with all appearances of interest.

"Actually getting married without benefit of urgency. Aha." Jack looking for Shirl's smile. Her faint puzzlement. Jack onward. "Do you know, I don't know anybody getting married these days. All my friends are living together. Taxes. Anna and I have just bought a house in Hampstead which we're redoing. Got it for twelve and it's worth at least fifteen already. More when we've finished. Actually, I don't think you should get married until you have children, do you?"

"Improve the honeymoon no end, I'm sure." Don't fun him Harry: *Observer* and BBC.

"Right." Now Mordecai with the lazy cigarette and the

loose look. "You see, we've been having an argument which you can settle." Jack smiling at Shirley and yearning to kiss her pale bright lips in her smooth face. Oh English cream and filtered sun. "What do you see in this painting, Shirley? What IS this painting?"

Op in the shop. Very pop. But no unkind words, bomb-thrower! BBC *Listener* and *Observer*.

Shirley beautifully on the spot. Mordecai leaning through his own smoke to intently listen. Nice of my bride to think.

"It's the Running Man."

"You see?" Jack throwing his attitude at Mordecai who still hasn't said a word through his wivering buttsmoke. "All they see is the iconography." And tossing red-lined away triumphant. Mordecai shrugging and going.

"What did I say wrong?" Dear Shirl in whose drawers I want to rummage.

"Come on upstairs and I'll show you." Walking away and her not. "Come on," brightly quietly. Putting her drink down on the mantel and actually coming.

"Here Shirl." Along this dusty back hall at the head of dim stairs and the huge seasound below decks there finally shut away. Or just enough to cover the rustle of Shirley cautiously looking in. The light at the back of her head. What the hell is in this room besides coats anyway? Typing table, chair. Where Nigel must do it.

"Where are we Harry?"

"I don't know. Mike found it. Come on in and close the door."

"Are you sure this is all right?"

"Of course not." Mmm. Pushing the door closed as I embrace you beautiful. But after her shy kiss her looking past me at the window.

"What are we going to do?"

"You sound frightened."

"If someone comes in?"

"Lucky them to see you sans."

"Harry. It's not our house." Quiet. "Are you taking off my dress?"

"Indeed." Bloody zip. Don't tear. There. And some dim windowlight. Never before this way. Never so eagerly with Shirl. "I love you." And slip off her slip against me actually half undressed here against me clothed. Oh to all of her. Slip gone.

"Really." But allowing with her arms nevertheless.

"Oh Shirley, so marvellous. You're so marvellous. I love you all." Gently patting me as if I am sick.

"Couldn't we lock the door?"

"Yes. I'll try." Nothing. Damn. A chair against. Shirl now limned in the window holding up her slip protective. Back five spaces.

"What's the matter?"

"I was afraid someone would hear you and come in."

"No. Never." Again against her. Damnable reluctance. Still clutching the slip against me her lover. "Shirl, please, I love you. I want to make love to you."

"I know."

"Well, what's the matter, then?"

"It's so awkward, here."

"But why, sweet, I've just jammed the door."

"What if they come in and find us?"

"Oh, damn them. They won't. Besides, you're beautiful. You should be seen."

"But not this way."

"Of course this way, sweet. How else?" Against her softness and gently disengage the slip once more. How many times. The slide of it up between us pressed together in the marvellous dim dark. But her cool kiss worrying the doorlight and sounds of footsteps voices coming. "Shh." Hugged together fearful. Oh to be discovered with her marvellousness and comic forever after in our married twilight that night in this room long ago.

"Shirley, I don't care love, you are so beautiful and warm

and all I want is you now" and I don't care and what does it matter as long as we are like this together. Off shirt and press against her talking away her fears and mine to feel her against my chest and just let me unfuckle this thing atop that keeps us apart at the back there Shirl and don't fight me but give in with warm love. Her little soft sounds still standing and off triumphantly with her topmost and slip richly my hands at each side down to the last strap band of her palmed hips. Stand away to do it and witness knickers. To the knees. Wool. Scratchy.

"Shirley. Knickers."

"It's May."

"May?"

"It's cold."

"But don't you care if I see you in these?"

"I don't mind if you do." Oh, lovely reply upending me.

"Someone. Coming in. Harry, it's so unpleasant here. Anyone could walk in at any moment. Don't you think."

"Jesus, it's the same everywhere in this bleeding country. No room inside because the parents don't approve, and you can't do it outside. What the hell, do we have to go to France to make love?"

"No, Harry, no, not at all. Don't be angry dear. When we go home. In the library."

"Well, it was the same in the country. Essex, Wessex, nosex, the three counties of England. And hell, your family is rich."

"Of course, that might be the trouble." And she looking at me with fun in her eyes to get at my colonial feelings. But biddy, you don't know what rich is, lying on the bare rocks bare to the sun in the north making love forever and swimming in the lake before and after, all to yourself, alone. There's even a song about it. But this dark moment is frustrated by our complex problems.

"You sit there knicker-naked like that how can I fail to want to, beautiful."

"I've been trying to get dressed." And in this moment of

17

frustration with the sense of impending love is the time to tell her. Do it in the gloom Harry, but first search out a cigarette you never smoke to scratch and light by flare of match from Nigel's writing desk covered with coats. Lighting an unfamiliar Gitane to tell her.

"Shirley, I've got bad news."

"What is it?" And no sense of surprise in her voice but the watchful calm of those who know about life, of Shirley who knows me.

"Your old man. Went and got a job for me." Smoking this huge Gitane which is too much for my poor burned lungs inhaling as I don't know how to do.

"Doing what?"

Anyway, the truth. Tell her. "I'm leaving."

"Leaving. Leaving, Harry? What do you mean?" Not the way I intended this at all.

"I mean, I can't go through with the job bit, and I can see what this means to your family, and I can't go through with the wedding. So there's nothing to do but get out."

Shirley looking up at me following with her eyes my face as I walk around the room, horribly I keep walking away ready for the darting door and gone, but stop, come back and face her.

"How did it start?" The puzzlement in her face is worse than hurt, because now I know I must explain, and can't just cut out as I wanted, and in the telling is the pain of blood. How my voice drones on with it all as death stands here in the broad evening light and no one sees him. And I've still got one on. Pressing my pants.

"Was it just the job, Harry, or what? I mean, you know that I can work."

"In the first place it was the job."

"Very evil beginning."

"Very evil. Photographer. Working in a goddamned photography studio for twelve pounds a week. I could hardly believe it. There was a ghastly aptness to it, from his point of view. Mine too, for that matter. But he was so pleased."

"What did you say? I must say, I wish I had seen you two at it."

"I didn't know what to say. He seemed to be expecting me to say thank you, and I could only think of the bottomless horror of it. I left that scene five years ago when I came over here, and now suddenly it's on me again. I just can't face it Shirl."

"Don't take the job."

"Sure, great. You know what'll happen then. We have to find a flat still, we have to pay the rent. That's why I was so upset when I gave up the studio. I mean, why I am so upset *now*. I afforded it then, and now, I can't get it back, and what are we going to do?" The big silence. Live with your mother and father. "You see what I mean, Shirl. We haven't really faced it, yet, and now that we have to face it, it's preposterous."

"I can work. We're not likely to suffer. You've been selling."

"But you know how your parents feel about that. It's not safe. It will be too hard on you."

"They'll let us make our own way."

"Oh no. Not after tonight. I've seen the whole ghastly thing suddenly outlined in crimson. Crimson of my own blood leaking away in something I hate. I can hardly believe we have been so late deciding this, but there it is. We have nowhere to live, unless we go back to your house. Yeah, and then one jolly little lump, with your old man hustling down to the city and the club every day with the rolled brolly, and me staring into the bottomless coffee cup at breakfast, constantly having to answer the question, and how come you didn't go out this morning at eight like a proper little bourgeois, H. Summers?"

"We'll get a flat right away. Take anything."

"You know why we have taken nothing. They're all so ridiculously expensive on what I make. Or else they're too depressing. I should never have let the studio go."

"We can live at home for a week or two, Harry, then we'll find something."

"It won't be to their taste, Shirl. I warn you, they will

come and inspect it, and they won't like it, and they'll probably offer to subsidize us to something better, and then they'll have a lien on us."

"What's a lien, darling?" To tell her, hearing the roar of London out the window, the surge of the party below. Rapids in the distance canoeing down the river falling silent paddling listening as the earth itself roars like a dragon.

"I'm supposed to go down there tomorrow. Talk to the guy. Take the job. I don't know how to get out of it."

"Just say no on the telephone."

"Then your old man will hold it against me later. 'I got him a job and he wouldn't take it and now look at him. Poor. Making my daughter poor.' "

"Lots of people start out poor. He knows that."

"You know what he thinks is poor? Thirty pounds a week. Shameful. 'Why does that boy keep blithering about his paintings when he could be making a decent screw like the rest of us.' "

"I can work. Come on, Harry, you're taking this so hard. It's not good for you. Let's go back and drink some of Nigel's champagne."

"Poverty and champagne. That'll be it, Shirl. There's another thing, it'll be worse for us even if we do get a flat and I go on this way, because there'll always be the reminder of what we're missing. Invites to Cowes when we can't afford the shoes let alone quids to get down and back. It's no good, Shirl, I see it all quite plainly. We have got to get out, and now, before the whole thing closes over us in a great big wave."

"Harry, darling you sound so desperate. I'm sure things aren't that bad yet. Come and sit down."

"Do you know what I felt tonight. Fear. Running away fear. I haven't for years. Coming here was my big break. I was getting away from all this. Now it's here again. The trap. Commercialism, indifference to life, the cozy attitudes, safeness, dullness, the ruin of inspiration. I was dying in Canada, Shirley, dying on my feet, I had that kind of job before, it's no good, I had that scene up to my ears, that's why I came away, and now it's surrounding me again all grey and awful, smothering me. I punched a clock, I worked in an advertising agency. I designed labels and milk bottle tops and TV ads. One day I was in the studio and everything was hairy, everything was going wrong, and I wanted to laugh because they were all so tense over trifles. It was a big deal, live, going on the air in a few minutes, and all of a sudden the producer came on the PA system he was hairy with rage he just shouted, he screamed 'move that asparagus half an inch to the left.' I thought, I don't have to take that, I don't have to waste my life doing that, and I just quit, right there, I just walked out, I got away, and it was the best thing I ever did. I went so fast I left a hundred bucks in pay. And I know what the other guys are doing now, they're back there moving the asparagus half an inch to the left for ulcers and lung cancer and mortgages and a new car and the boss yelling at them day after day. Because they didn't have the guts to quit. They all hated it. It's a world I never made and I'm not going back to it."

"No." Scarcely even accepts that. Just is part of it as I am, and thinks.

"We have to go. Now."

"Oh." Long painful sigh out of her. "When?"

"Now. Tonight, this minute, go."

"Without anything?"

"Few clothes, some paint. Go."

"But Harry, why now, this instant?"

"Because afterwards, it will be too late."

"We can still go. There's no law that says we have to stay."

"The law is fear, I feel it already, I'm afraid already, and any minute it will be too late. Already I feel myself giving in, now to you. I'm desperate Shirl, I've got to go while I've got the guts." Terrible confession, terrible urgency to go.

"Or I never will." The flat statement committing me without her. Now the silence comes round us like a bell cutting off everything. I've got to go and she with me. Her equal silence sitting there thinking unable to come unable to go.

"Will you come?"

Spoken into the night-drumming silence. She can't possibly say yes. She's not the kind. Come Shirley. Sitting frozen unable to speak. The sudden agony of her face filling with terrible thoughts. Feeling your pain with hope Shirley. Oh I am sorry.

Still silent.

"Shirley?"

Whispering. "I'll come. But afterwards. Not now, Harry, not now."

"You will." And it is done. Suddenly Shirley weeping alone on the chair and me unable to go to her but going. Standing. Defensive. "Don't cry Shirl."

"Harry, you are asking so much. It's so hard on me." Her left hand wiping her forehead.

"I'm sorry."

"I don't know how you can be this way, just after we . . . just when we are like this" and her sudden gold coolness and lushness still half undressed in the windowlight. The very print of her smooth alley still pressed on my finger, and yes she is right.

"A housing shortage doesn't make you less lovely, Shirl."

"Oh for God's sake, you're so sententious. You know that's not what I meant." The madness in me is what she means. Don't face it, H. Summers. Number 109659. "I'd better go. As soon as I get somewhere, a few days, only, just get away and call you."

"I can't leave them. Not now. It would hurt them so much, I can't Harry."

"I know. I understand."

"How can you? You're just leaving this way. When? Now?"

Unable to deny it. Wanting now to stay. Must keep my mind. Made up. "I love you." I think.

"Oh," and the agony of the sound. She doesn't believe.

"Don't, don't. I better go." Shirley refusing to look at me. Holding her as she stands unresponsive.

"Why?" Unable to go on.

"I feel so badly. I'm sorry." Uselessly patting her.

"It feels as if you're running away from me." Patting me back.

"I'm not Shirley, I'm not. I swear . . ." Convincing. "In a day, just a couple of days, anywhere. France first, Paris, somewhere. Maybe Ghana. Just away. I can't help it Shirl, I just can't help it. I'm broken. You don't know how I feel. It's just horrible for me. I can't explain properly. Just go. Just got to go, keep moving, get away."

"All right all right stop, I can't stand it anymore. Just stop Harry." Viciously turning away, back to me. Fists. Stopping herself. I'm frozen. No more to her. Don't hurt, Harry.

Walking away. Still not looking at me. Whispering. "I don't want you to leave me, Harry." Cornered. Looking at me. Your face awful in passion at me. Shake my head. "No, no." Shake my head. Out the door. Leaving it open.

God a terrible scene. To have made her look like that, sweating and red, composure gone. The terrible face of need, love. Unsayable. Shirley draining me into herself, clutching at me, and me giving her. Hang on, hang on, first round gone, bell for the second, just hang on. I can still win it.

Now in a sense wrecked. In a sense, free, and running. Keep going Harry. How to go? Where to go? Shirley's? Rich house. No more to steer to it on a sleety night. But go. With the shameful cheques cashed on our joint account.

This bedroom loaned to me for the duration of the wedding hostilities. With my door as closed as I can. That Aunt Marge will not come in now. The few essentials of my painting life. Footsteps. Aunt Marge. Who? Knock at the door.

Tiptoeing to the cupboard. Gently in. My God, the packing. But she will think it is for Antibes. Luckily haven't told her where.

"Harold?" Gently. Marge. Holding breath. If she opens the cupboard door, and I half-undressed. Her pacing about in there. What is she doing, dear and gentle old codface. As she opens the cupboard door and lights me full up. Eyes my exposed moneybelt.

"Oh excuse me." What expression to give her. As she politely begins to close the door. Coffin lid pops up, corpse is smoking cigar. Incredible. Marge politely half-shuts door, leaving me ajar. Now I to open it? Yet unable to emerge but stand here among clothes watching her with back turned tidying my room.

"Good morning."

"Good morning Harold. I'm sorry to disturb you."

"Not at all."

"Are you all ready?"

And ready for what, dear Marge. Have you keepers out the door just for me?

Nice morning slept well. Uncle Billy Well Well Well. Shirley. All the while terribly tempting to just lay lightly one finger on tie rack here on door back and slowly hook it back over my face talking the while as she finishes tidying and lets herself out.

I must go today. Must be today. Cannot stand any more of this fantastic secrecy. Whereabouts must remain private.

"Good-bye for now Harold."

"A tout à l'heure, Aunt Marge."

And she is going. Gone. Out and down the stairs. Must finish the packing trying not to think of poor Shirl. Everything I put in here is one of the bricks I am using to seal myself up so they will not find me. Shirley, believe me, I do not want to do it. You are lovable beyond belief but I am foxed. Love, I am now cutting your strings and every one hurts and every one is not the last. Christ. I can hardly see the box for the mist in my eyes. Refusing to weep. It is the best and only thing. Sketch book. Six new empty ones. Charcoal pencils. The small plywood panels instead of the great canvasses I have lately had. Well, it was time for a change anyway, and I can find other studios. Close them. Tiptoe to the lavatory. The two small bags. Out the window. Jesus, I forgot this roof is slate.

Tile. Impractical. Just have to sneak it down the dark back-stairs. Check everything. Oxfords. Grey bags. Jacket. Mack. Hatless into the void.

One dark step here at a time while they are beyond the two doors into the dining room. That Marion does not hear. To the tradesmen's door at the landing. Bucket. Damn. Oh that incredible noise. Over and over down. Never stopping out the door into the drive down and round the Macready's hedge. Mud. Run. Down the street running like a hare. Oh never see me kind and understanding people, do not now look out and see the pitiful spectacle of Harry Summers fleeing his aunt and uncle and Shirley and all the little Summers running in the twilight street of early London spring with two bags flapping and the windows flying up as he hits each square of pavement running shouting hold stop I say running breathless round the corner for the little pause and the heartbeats whacking me to stop and now to sedately walk as if the police bells were all finished and Ramsden Park Road had seen me every night at six before. Easy to the corner and on to the twenty-six bus to Brixton? No, gaol. Airport. Off we go. They'll have all the exits stopped up by this time tomorrow. Glamorous thou art, and cowardly, and shalt be what the weird sisters promised in the set-sail hereafter.

Boom, the bus doors close. Out of it like a punished rogue. No more the glamour of the hunting and punting set. But into the great infinity to turn my regrets into causes.

"What is your destination sir?"

"Eh, um, Canada."

"Yes sir. Any particular city? May I see your ticket?"

"Oh, I need one."

"Just over there sir." They say a plane takes off here every twenty-six seconds. Must be room on one for old Harry. Canada? My God no.

"Paris. I would like a ticket to Paris."

"Yes sir."

What has a man but his friends. Friends with God. I remember at camp singing *Abide with Me* under the trees at night on the shore with the campfire going. And where has that gone. Down into some hole in me. Now for André's place. At least he is in this French city. Appreciates the canoe as a work of art and compromise as the way of life. To that damned grey Place de l'Opéra which always defeated me because I was so unruly and therefore never able to get the scratch to live like the damned rich. Cook's, American Express along the east side as I remember. They have washed Paris it said but it still looks dirty to me. As I must now look, after my unshaven air-sickness on the plane. The rough channel crossing is a cliché come true. Half my life I have spent trying to avoid making clichés come true, and now I expand one into the air. So tiring in this day descended from the Franks and Visigoths via Charlemagne and Churchill. At least the white cliffs of Dover are dishtowel grey. Yes they are, Anglophiles of little Ontario towns such as home. Port Faith.

Now we walk along with the moneybelt tight, the dunnage bag still ungainly under my right arm this treed street leading eastish from the Place. The Bon Marché as ever. The shopping bags. Blue taxis. Now along to the restaurant with the dreadful cafeteria breakfasts we used to have there. Selling dollars on the black-market to our seven-foot-tall Algerian in yellow shoes that squeaked, as I remember. To the short street with the one café and the grey stone teetery buildings about and the hotel with the elevator on a shiny brass pole. André's door. Beside the café. But Madame awaits behind her guichet-desk.

"Bonjour, m'sieur'dame." Aha, the singing words of the Midi. A kindly concièrge for André. Langage de plaisir.

"Bonjour madame. I'm looking for M. Riancourt."

"Oh, he has left."

"Left, when?"

"He went with his wife. So nice."

"Yes, when?"

"Loupio comes with the fish on Wednesday, it was the day

after, today is Friday, it was eight days ago, m'sieur." And her smile as she produces the accurate memory. I love you lady. I bet you count up tediously in old francs too.

"But when is he coming back." And the shrug. Maybe never.

"Where did he go then. Trouay? Spéracèdes?"

"I don't know m'sieur. You are a friend of his? From Paris?"

"I'm his friend from London."

"Oh, anglais. Yes, he went to Canada. He left for Montreal, I believe. That's it. With Madame Riancourt, for Montreal. Il fait froid là-bas, eh?" The old French question again.

"Oui, évidemment. Couche de neige de cinq mètres en ce moment. Fin de mai. Did he go quickly, or what?"

"He just packed his bags and they went. He said he would write to me."

"Has he written?"

"No, m'sieur. Not yet."

"I see."

"He did not write to you?"

"No."

"Excusez-moi un tout petit second, m'sieur, je m'occupe . . . ne quittez pas . . ." Into the telephone, second receiver clapped to her other ear.

André gone, Janine gone. Goodbye goodbye, Madame. So oddly. Not coming to London, not telling us, no letter about our wedding. Gone back home. Canada, dear old Grannyda. Five years, Harry, five years gone. Was he getting lonely like you?

Au revoir to madame on the phone behind the glass door now and outside. With my two dunnage bags dragging in the blue French air of Paris full of moto noise and fumes and stink of shit in the gutters and Gauloises from the cafés and fresh bread. This langage de plaisir de France. Sun burning the planiers and ourselves on shadowy red sand under the trees last summer playing boule full of music and wine. Was he wondering about home then. We scarcely talked about it. Where is home for us?

27

Down the street Harry. Lots of pounds round the old belt zipped safely in. Shirley's face printed alive on all the Queen's notes saying take it all Harry, but why don't you take me too Harry.

A coffee in the sun or a pastis? Last chance in France. Here at the carrefour. Must decide. Big red and silver plane.

the
lonely
ones

In the Rapids

Down the rapids, or the portage? Stand for a minute in the woods listening. They sound high, very high.

What's the date? – about June. High water. Very loud from here.

André has left it there as always. A lot of broken branches round here, footmarks on the path and now he has made room for at least two canoes, maybe three. And this one is new. High up where the bears can't eat it.

Lift it down gently, onto the shoulder roll and take it through the woods. It'll be the rapids. No matter how high they are.

Brilliant green of the springtime woods around me. View of the world from underneath a canoe, the long dark point riding ahead like a roof over the narrow forest trail. Wide as a deer's rump, André said. Wide as a canoe's thwarts.

First time in what, four years, I have shouldered a canoe. Once the ambition to get one sent over to Ktos and paddle down from the Piraeus out to my island.

Can this be the right trail? It seems much longer than before, when we shot the rapids that time in August laughing and falling out at the end into the falls and sliding over laughing and holding a wine bottle and bouncing down the smooth

29

long slope of the rocks full of nothing.

But it is the trail. The last long root-tangled descent to the edge. There it is twenty feet down and going fast. Branches pulled sideways in the flood, swept fast downriver now, black silent water slithering there. Long living snake of water sliding. Pulling the leaves down sideways, hissing. And halfway down the rapids, the arena, whitewater, rocks like animals in the arena snarling charging from every side, the terrible noise. Chute Bruyante they call it round here because the noise is trapped in these high red Laurentian walls and never seems to leave. Even in winter that time when we snowshoed in you could hear the soft turn of the water under the long ice and open here and there sliding past black and cold and hissing along the edge of the ice where the deer had come down to drink.

Just gently down the slope. Tie the bowline here. The two paddles, one lashed in, throw in your dunnage bag and get in gently so. The little red canoe rocking on the fast water with the bowline hanging on to the cedar trunk. Is it strong enough? I really should walk the water first.

It is at least intelligent and not afraid to do this walking down the trail on the steep bank hardly ever used because no one ever comes this way. Everyone uses the portage, Harry. The Chute Bruyante is impassable.

And from here in June in a high sun, they certainly look bad. White everywhere, roaring everywhere spring flood.

Jesus, maybe I should portage. But I have never done this, I have never in my life gone and done such a dangerous and difficult thing before, such a beautiful thing worth doing but not I admit worth dying for but then I intend to do it and not die for it: did I intend to die for the asparagus job at the ad agency in Toronto? No I did not and there I might have had a heart attack and it was not even worth doing let alone worth thinking about dying for, and this at least is a sensationally beautiful thing to do and the water is leaping at me full of joy, come in Harry come on in and try us and see what we're like, impossible, I can't believe that, and there is the water racing and roaring and yelling come come come Harry, those waves don't know Daddy drowned, drowned in June in 1944 off France on D-Day June dying and drowning and gone. But I will not die here I'll get through walking back to the canoe looking at all that and knowing I am about to do it, it is impossible and here we are one.

Going fast now knees up water roaring, grab water sideways, paddle, grab, too fast, water too fast, can't control can't keep up to it must dig, catch up to the river still alive pointing down not sideways get going paddle faster paddle out rockahead gonepast left, left there deep trout pool past the gravel now again steep rapids, more downrace crazy can't stop mile of white water here racing past me wind in ears roar in ears mile of white water racing under me canoe too fast racing under me rocks past bounce crash god rock through bottom not through, saw the ribs bulge, now ahead dark turning place after the long race and the falls ahead, make it round the fast roaring corner here steep trees high over me reach far out to the right black deep water backed up racing here pulling me over the falls I'll die here, this is my death pulling falls coming oh God we're high fly out flying out flying down, sliding oh beautiful falling sliding never stop sliding down all my life sliding down the falls crashing into water. Crashed onto flat black water whirlpooling turning dizzy watching falls turn round and round above me, the falls go by the woods go by the stream goes by the falls go by there is water in the canoe but it is not growing we are not sinking.

What did I do?

Did I come down there? Paddle to the bank. Hold on and watch. The huge white roaring falls. Looking back up over the pool, the rapids falling down from above like huge white stairs towards me constantly moving better get back or they'll slide all the way down here and get me the spray rising into the sunlight and birds flying through it trees falling and leaning and growing into that wet sunlight over the river. My God that's a steep rapids, did I really come down all that race of water and rock? the huge falls here swaying and falling, water bulging over the edge shining swinging like hair falling. Height of falls approximately eight feet, reason I got over it the solid pour of water racing me down. Safest time of year to shoot is now.

In the explosion of white water beating at the smoothed rocks, one sandpiper stands on a rock on legs like two hairs watching the scene around.

Hey, I made it, hey I made it André. Where are you now, waiting at the cabin? No one has built on the lake I hope. Just us again out here, all alone.

A warm summer day to come back Harry. Yes indeed. Down the long river two miles now deep in June full of bugs sweeping back and forth the birds flying and nesting. Bluejay there, sharp singing in the woods, whitethroat, song sparrow, maybe a hermit thrush later on. The hummingbird at that portage once just in there passing the landing place. I've at least saved myself that long boring portage. But the balsam smells nice on that trail. Little coloured bird hanging over the portage resting place at the end by the water, always seen in country gardens and never in the bush before. Canada jay there calling. Lovely place here André. You picked well.

It is elegant to float down this river under the trees joined above your head. I am sweating wet, or is it spray or is it both? Should stop and bail this sloshing canoe. Really should. Shine of a little beach down there. Watch the bottom, no rocks all sand. In autumn come the moose, trumpeting through here, and it is dangerous to come down this drybed stream only three feet deep then instead of eight as now with trout shining all around, because they just charge through the water looking for the does and if you are in the way, bam, like a rock in the rapids, it just goes right through you and goodbye you in the cold water one October night.

Yesterday I was in Paris today I am on the river remembering moose stories pulling into shore to bail my canoe after the rough passage down the Chute Bruyante. Incredible. Did my jet pass this far north circling to land at Dorval?

Slide the bow gently up there and step forth to lift the rest of us up and stand in the sun drying a bit as we tip her over on her side and let the water and accumulated sanddust of last fall spill out the gunwales. Through the gunwale holes nails of water stab the sand leaving craters in line, of mysterious origin to archaeologists. Sixteen spotted sandpipers pissing in formation.

Nearly to the marsh here. Might see a heron or two. Or is that a heronry in the dead tree there. Black bushes of nests hanging in the old dead grey tree. Maybe so. Probably beaver runs in there and the herons are standing in the runs stiff-legged fishing.

I thought I turned right here and went on out into the lake, but I guess I go further down and yes, there they are past those little rock reefs and then right and down the long open lake towards the high hump of André's island. Yes, that's it. The last time there was fall, about what, six years ago, yes and we came down in the canoe and it was cold and grey and wet and blowing.

The final surge out the river mouth and the shallow beaches here, the sand island where you can't build for the floods of autumn and spring, the little grey remembered reefs where we came to swim and skindive those times and made our picnics naked on the rocks lying in the sun.

How far it is down the lake, I didn't remember the lake so long and wide, the hills so big. This canoe is a slow way of going. Yesterday walking up the jet cabin to my seat I stepped the length of this lake with each stride. Hills flying today, clouds blue shadows moving over them, sudden lightning of the sun on a whole range of hills green after the cloud shade, race of white water clouds in the blue river of air, green of the trees toplit by the sun blackshadowed under, covering the slopes, filling the valleys lining the lakeshore, shaved by fire far over there in a flat sloped field; on the irregular hills' high horizon, a regular line cool against the pale lower sky like fur clothing the earth.

From here impossible to make out the island against the far shore five miles down the lake, the water now calmed flat and lying out silverblue as I crawl over it, one canoe with me in it pushing primitively with my stick at the water. To catch a fish and take it on down to him at the cabin.

Will Janine be there? Black-haired nervous lovely, my friend able to cope with me and André simultaneously. Admirable girl.

Push this loaded old thing downlake over the flat water now too hot for me sun glaring up heat from a stovehole. Yes, the old woodstove inside the door. Come on Harry, push this old barge along.

Now the island shows, shoreline slightly below the far shore. Against the far trees, possible to see the opening now to the narrow channel around behind the island. And there's the dock, grey streak under the trees. He may even be watching me come down the lake now. Give him the loon call with my hands to my mouth covering the lake with its echoing shake.

No response.

Glide in here by the dock. But no boat. No canoe. He must be gone. For the day?

Better go up and check anyway. The old grey dock strung out here dark under the overhanging cedars. A few needles lying on it. Seems deserted. Has anyone been here yet this year? Stay a day or two with my own food.

Quietly lift the canoe onto the dock. Up the path. Now there's a strange thing. Someone has been here. Branches on the winding path cut. Sharp butts left by secateurs. Quietly up the path in case.

Soon see it through the trees. If it is still there and it is, standing beyond, see you grey and old there and a window and the sun hot and bright in the clearing before. André. There he is.

"André." Call him and wave coming to the clearing's edge.

Stand still. What's the matter?

"André?"

"Harry. It's Harry. Don't shoot." Janine screaming running down the verandah. "Harry Harry Harry, thank God, don't shoot, it's Harry," Janine running wildly arms flying down the steps across the clearing to me.

"Oh Harry," face ecstatic hitting me holding me kisses cheeks holding, André shambling forward. What's in his hand? Walkie-talkie?

"Harry. Excuse me." Holding his arms out too. Embrace both cheeks. His beard on my ear. Janine holding me still.

"What is this?"

André sad eyes glancing up into the woods. Now comes a man out of the wood carrying a rifle and a long aerial. Pushing it back into a small walkie-talkie as he comes. Medium height, black hair, taut look. Stands apart. Looks at André who still watches him. Speaks.

"Who is he?" Meaning me.

"A friend."

"C'est un Anglais."

"A friend, Langevin. My oldest friend."

"What is he doing here? How did he find you?"

André turning to me.

"I used to come here years ago. We came all the time sketching. André, what is this?"

"We are mixed up in one hell of a thing, that's for sure. But how did you know I was here, Harry."

"I called your mother in Montreal. She said you had gone up north painting, so I knew where you would be."

"But you didn't even know he was back in Canada. He has only been here two weeks." Langevin curt.

"Well, of course, I knew he was in Paris, I went to see him. The concièrge told me he'd gone. Are you going to shoot that thing eh?" And smile, mocking his rifle among friends. Langevin coolly unembarrassed watches me. Here is an enemy.

"I don't understand, André. Shoot someone? Here? Shoot a man just walking up here?"

"Maybe. You could have been a policeman, Mountie." Janine breaks away and goes and sits in the shade with sad dark eyes watching me from the steps.

"But what is happening?"

"Harry, maybe you'd better go."

"I just came."

Langevin finally puts down the gun. How strange I want to be introduced properly to this man who has just had my head in his sights walking up the path. "Of course, pleased, nothing personal old man, not at all. Good shot." Cough. Dead.

"How did you get here?"

"You saw me."

"No, we did not."

"How could you miss me then. I paddled across the lake."

"I mean, did you see anyone on the portage." His glance at André.

"No. I didn't take the portage." And André suddenly smiles, he knows. "Hey, André, I made it, I . . ."

"You came down the rapids." He is impressed. Hand on my arm watching me. "Harry. You're mad."

"Yeah, it was terrific. Never saw anything like it in my life."

Langevin staring at me. "You shot La Chute Bruyante?"

"Yes. Just now. Come on, I'll take you through if you like."

A smile he can't help on Langevin's stiff face. "That's why we didn't hear from Jeannot." And suddenly Janine laughing beautifully on the verandah, leaning against the little post watching us and laughing. "Harry, you're wonderful. Come in and have some coffee. Tell us all about it."

Still not knowing, walking into the cool cabin. The smell. Woodsmoke, old cedar and pine drying in the walls. No new furniture. Stone fireplace in the middle. Old brown kitchen chairs. Hey, and the red can of Hero fire extinguisher on the wall. Challenging André to drink it that night we were out of beer. Car pennants from Ausable chasm. But that is new. The oil on the tongue and groovy cedar walls. "Tongue and groovy, remember André, the Hero joke." Janine standing by the green cast iron hand-pump where we would idly pump up the water from the lake talking and letting it overflow onto our bare feet on the floor watching it go out the door and down the steps as she pumps now standing there against the light in black corduroys and pale white soft shirt. And André in huge thick bush shirt too hot for today but good against the god-damned flies. With the screens up looking out at the heat of the day and Langevin arguing, still making problems for both of us.

I was here on this lake, in this cabin, before you ever saw it, Langevin whoever the hell you are, I helped build this place and by God I am staying. But what if André has gone and robbed a bank or something. Stalin in Tiflis-sur-lac, Bonnie and Clyde down the main drag of Saint Tit. Shooting back at the pursuers.

Still on the verandah arguing, finally coming in.

"Excuse me, I must go." Langevin past me into the back bed-rooms and back in a moment with a grey dunnage bag over his shoulder.

"Tomorrow."

"Tomorrow."

"And speak to Jeannot. Tell him what Harry did."

"I will."

Langevin finally turning at the door. Actually formally says au revoir to me.

"Au revoir."

And gone down the path hearing his footsteps on the hot pine needle path past the cabin side down to the lake.

"How will we get back, André?"

"There's another canoe hidden."

"Who is Jeannot?"

"He was stationed with a set halfway down the portage, you know where the old lumber road comes in. We never thought anyone would shoot the rapids especially this time of year. So it seemed better to guard the road and the portage simultaneously, you see."

"But why?"

"Ah, yes." Janine laughing. Watching us two.

"Is it this Separatist thing, bombs and everything?"

"That's it." André looking suddenly relieved. Langevin gone, André enthusiastic. "Harry, you remember how we talked in France, eh? Not our country, for me, and England not yours. Yes, well, here, this is a revolution, and I came home to it. Back home to my country. This is my Refus Global. I came back to our republic to kick out the Anglos. You too, Harry. Out. That's what Langevin was saying, by invitation only. A grand opening. Début of a nation. I am the new minister of anti-culture." Very happy long face, ancient beard with an owl in it. Long boney form in his blue bush shirt and the bad teeth. Long arms airing about the room with that jerky action of his.

"What are you talking about?"

"We all came home. This is the newest part of the world. I got a Canada Council grant to travel, so I came home on it. The bastards will probably sue me in court. Quebec, saviour of the dying west. We are all home again. Like lemmings we shall plunge over the cliff to our destruction, probably."

Thin blue-green eyes narrowing on to me here with this political argument as once in this room years ago on art and painting. Pointing at me with his André Riancourt drama. "Janine. A spy. Merde. In our very midst. Spy for the detested tourists. Janine, poison his tea. No, wait, let me indoctrinate him first, then put him to a slow and ravaging death for the sins of his forefathers. What have you to say before you die, tourist. Goddamned English. Harry, mon copain. You look distressed. What is the matter?"

"I don't understand. This nationalism."

"You are a visigoth, barbarian from without the sacred borders, interloper, thiever of babies in the night, swindler, bum, tourist, trampler on the sacred soil of Quebec. From now on, you shall need a passport in French to get on a subway car. And I swear to you by the antiquity of our friendship on this lake, in this room, not a hair of your head shall be harmed, and not a square stone of your artless buildings left one upon the other. We are reclaiming our soul, and you shall bow down and be grateful for it. Money-maker, American." Watch him carelessly. "You shall come with your millions to gaze upon the Parthenon we are building and not a sou of ten times what you own will buy you a dog's understanding of its perfect merit.

One Holy Catholic Apostolic Revolution." And alive with laughter falling onto the couch under the red Hero can laughing at his rhetoric. "It's all propaganda, Harry and all deadly serious. Have some Hero, Anglo."

"What is this Anglo bit?"

And Janine full of it now, and mocking him. Her eyes seem hurt by this, somehow, she is not with it: "It's homecoming week, Harry. Hate Ontario week again. He is one part Picasso, one part Jesus, and one part Che Guevara."

"Two Latins and a Semite, what do you say to that, Anglo?"

"André, what is this Anglo bit? You know my mother is French, as if it matters anyway." André's surprised look at me. "André, I told you that years ago."

"Ah yes, yes you did. Worse for you then. You're vendu."

This is incredible.

"But Harry, you also told me your family was toute anglicisée."

"She speaks French, my mother. Where do you think I learned? Her maiden name is Lamorandière. She was born in Quebec."

"You also told me once that your instincts were English, that you thought completely as an Anglo. What did you think when you saw Langevin coming out of the woods, eh?"

"That he intruded upon friendship. With that goddamned rifle." All eyes on it standing upright in the corner where Langevin has put it. André hurt; can't help it. Help him, Harry, soften it for him. "Nevertheless, I wanted to be introduced to him properly even while he was standing there. 'How do you do, how do you do, ça tire, oui ça tire bien, if you get my satirical pun.' Very Anglo of me, eh? Cool in the face of danger. Introduction to the enemy."

"Yes." He does smile, accepting.

"Anyway, to think as an Anglo is to believe in the French in this country. And how could I escape that?"

André now walking round the room watching the lake where Langevin paddles away. "If you can believe that Harry, you can believe anything, including our right to survive. And so maybe it is not too late to save you, eh?" Takes a cup of coffee from Janine and watches me, sipping it.

"To save me?"

"To save ourselves."

"The artist as messiah. I don't believe that, André."

"But who else? I must help. Business, politics, the whole establishment virtually is sold out. We have to abandon the pleasures of art for a while, to save ourselves. Harry, it was you who taught me this in Trouay last year. You can't fight it now."

"At Trouay? Thank you, Janine, just sugar please."

"Yes. You told me that you believed the artist owed a debt to society which he almost invariably had to play out as a revolutionary. You said it was part of the fate of the artist. Remember, you quoted Picasso, something about not living in an ivory tower, but art being a different means of carrying on the struggle." As he talks and I hear all the old words I indeed told him, watching Langevin down the lake disappearing into the heat shimmer.

Grab the rifle suddenly from the corner, sight in on Langevin. He is small against the crosshairs, thin as the sighting lines. To send a couple over his head to make sure there is no ricochet, and then watch him paddle with fear. Put up the rifle. André stands there, tense, afraid of what I am doing. But he is saying nothing. He finally trusts his friendship more than his fears of Anglo nationalism. "If you were convinced, André, you never would have left the rifle there, never would have let me put down the coffee cup, never would have let me cross the room to the window with the rifle and aim it at one of your soldiers."

"Harry, for Christ's sake. What are you saying?"

"That you instinctively trust friendship more than the revolution. That, André, you are just like me au fond, people, your personal relations, your friends matter more to you than art, politics, the revolution, death."

He is not ready for that. He knows his answer but he will not tell me standing there in front of one of his own superb paintings alive as I have always seen him with the vague look of his blue eyes charged, and face now hardened by his conviction, his arguments against me and the political world. "Ah, Harry, I don't know what to say. On one level, that is true, on another, not. You will see, you will understand more soon."

The windows all open let us hear the Canada jay. His long clear call rising from the clearing down there, usually gone by this time of day. Likes to sing early in the morning. "I'm glad we've still got the bird. Or is he a new one?"

Janine getting sandwiches. André thinking. Me seated at the old brown wooden painted kitchen table – didn't I paint these legs with the curling red leaves and flowers, yes they are still here. Janine gently watching me now thinking.

"Harry, you haven't told us. Where is Shirley?"

As we always used to do here, lying on the flat rock under the pine at the corner of the island looking up the lake to the west with a case of Molson's *Bleu* and some wine, lying on your back in the pine needles with just enough wind over us to keep cool and blow off the flies, on the green moss brilliant like a frog's back.

"Harry, I used to think you were perfect." André sidelying looking out head on elbow up the lake, glancing across at me to smile as he drives in a joke, swigging back a beer cold from the lake with a burp. "You even wanted to marry England. Now how will you get into the House of Lords?"

"André, I'm ruined, and you talk like that."

"How, ruined, Harry?" Janine sitting back against the long grey drift log hot in the sun in her black maillot pretty legs soft on the rock, turning to look up at me against the sun with her hand to her eyes. Softly move my shadow over you.

"Yes, Harry. One unfortunate love affair is nothing. Remember Césare? He had three before twenty. Wanted to kill himself before he was twenty-one. World's record, I think." Sips at the beer and smiles.

41

"André, my oldest, my best friend, I tell you I am ruined, and you sit there with an owl in your beard, laughing at me."

"What's killing you?"

"Today is my wedding day."

"Go back. She is rich and delicate, you are poor and gross. A perfect match. I advise you to go back. You want to marry her."

"Not any more." What is a lie?

"Yes, you are definitely mad. Now you will be common by choice as well as by birth."

"Your soupstained arrogance." Too hot here. Get up and unshirt to tan in the sun. Janine seeing my pink-money belt appear. Undo it and drop it casually with the shirt. Janine, you are not taking sides but letting it happen just now. What are you thinking? Your lips fly in your face like wings, lover.

"You could go back. You are obviously not convinced yet. But you have really run away. Mad."

"I know, I know." God, if it were all over and I free again.

"I thought you weren't coming because you disapproved. You could have come and supported me."

"Now Harry, that's not logical. I would have been there to advise you. Then you would have hated me."

"Why?" I must not sulk with him. Janine always notices it and hates it. Probably thinks it is my girlish way of undermining her girlish way with him. But her face is shining with sympathy now. She wants to talk. Look at her. "Janine, what should I do?"

"Oh Harry, I feel so sorry for you. André, you are being too hard."

"Anyone desperate enough to need advice is beyond taking it."

"Swim." Get up and race in, throw off frustration with a yelling dive into the clear Lac Diamant. Under and down into the winter frost hiding down here, up and blow silver into the air. André, Janine up sideways lying watching me, laughing. "Come on in, it's freezing. Feels great." Under and down again and a fast crawl out to the outmost blue turning black under me flying crawlstroke over the black air, under the shoreless sky. In the flat water atop, sunstruck, stay warm. Not so cold as below. Lying sculling back with the sun shining all over me keeping warm. Out on the dripping rocks splashing up towards them shaking waterdrops from my long blond hairs over André. Laughing at me, shoving a beer up at me. This good place.

I am alone in this. Janine can say nothing to me though I know she feels it. André wants only to mock it, put it away from him as he put away his own pain with girls in Montreal when he was starting out. Darkness. Darkness is the time to think of you Shirl. Mosquitoes still around. Almost eleven o'clock and still a bit of light in the sky to the west. Amazing. Shove off the canoe and paddle out fast away from the mosquitoes. Under the fantastic stars. As you look, more seem to come; where blackness was, more stars arrive. The moon's curved edge sharp over the hill and low. Black water with a chain of silver on its rippled edge. And a genuine loon somewhere singing into the hills. From another lake another loon calls him back, or is it the echo? Or is it a wolf howl far off there?

All the afternoon talking it out, lying in the sun, sleeping under the pine tree, in and out of the water, beer and swimming and talking. To lie back on the paddle blade now gazing up. Smoke a Gauloise and think of André and Janine, happy at the dinner table with a bottle of red and some hamburger meat from La Victoire down the road. A ten mile walk to the store, if the car breaks down. Tomorrow we must get in and go back to Montreal. How far we are away, and today I saw jet trails hung over us in the sky. Shirl, you should have come, you should be here now. This is what I wanted to do for our honeymoon, not your cousin's villa at Antibes, all dressup and crowded and museums, and people watching and ugly women in bikinis on the beach and homosexuals prowling the plage for homosexuals prowling the plage, and must be grateful to your cousin and to your family for making us conform comfortably, for making us do what they like to do. A life like whipped cream on stone.

If we could have come here, then we would have been happy. Just out here and live here one summer gradually falling in love completely, painting and drinking and loving and lying in the sun and loving and lying out naked on the rocks and painting you endlessly, Shirley in the bath, Shirley drying, Shirley in love, Shirley after love, Shirley in a canoe, Shirley under the pines in a big hat with nothing on. Shirley cooking, Shirley asleep under the pine tree, and the lake stretching away at her feet. Shirley the artist's English mistress wife lover friend and model, at the island the glorious summer they ran away from all that. Shirley's face looking at the view. God if I'd known then Shirley, I would have told you. Honestly, I would have told you. I did not know I wanted this so much with you until I followed André and Janine, here. And tomorrow we must get going again. I need to come to rest, somewhere.

"You can stay if you like Harry. It's just that I have to meet Langevin and some of the others tonight in Montreal. It still takes three hours to drive down from here, you know. So we have to go right after breakfast."

"Are you leaving any painting gear?"

"No. We'll have to take out the printing press another time. We haven't got time today."

"I see. I think I'll come out with you now, and then come back later maybe, next week, if you like. Help you take out the press."

"Well. Yes. Perhaps." André uneasy about me helping move the stolen press. "Harry, this is serious. I'm not just fooling around."

"Neither am I André. I meant it. I'll help you move the stuff back to Montreal. When you get a place."

"But why should you? I'm sorry." André realizing the question. Yet it is a good one.

"Come on you two." Janine standing sad-eyed behind him, dishes all cleared, arms down waiting. "We'll be late." Close the front door. No lock. Carry the bags down to the canoe. Three into it and across the lake. Faint cloud today. What time is it? About eleven, I guess. Always up late here, except when we're going somewhere up the lakes, and then we're out of the pit at sunrise.

To the portage landing and the day is too warm now to stay in the sun. Our few bags onto the sand here. Bloody sand flies hitting us as we stand here.

"I'll take it André." But he lifts the canoe and strides away. Janine with a couple of bags in the rucksack. Me with two little bags on the packboard. André gone up the trail.

"He is mad for this Separatist thing." Together with this beautiful girl up the northwoods trail.

"I know. I see you are not enthusiastic."

"It's a disaster. It is destroying us both."

"When did it start?"

"Months ago. In Paris, with friends from Montreal and Quebec. I almost did not come back to Canada with him." Janine firmly walking up the trail not looking at me, telling the path at her feet as she leans forward into the little pack-load on her back. One hand up fanning away the mosquitoes from her face. Pink sunburn from yesterday.

"You saw how he treated you at first. It has been the same with all his friends if they do not agree with him. It is an obsession with him. He has not painted anything for months."

"That oil on the wall at the cabin was new."

"That was from Trouay with you and Shirley last year. He has done absolutely nothing since. A few charcoal things of me at the lake. Nothing else."

"I'm sorry Janine."

"When we get back to Montreal, I don't know what will happen." Janine angry, afraid, needing advice and comfort, and yet, walking up the path, what can I say? What do I know? "I don't believe any of it anymore." Janine's firm statement.

Slogging heat. Back up the hill with the mosquitoes still at us and the green-backed flies. Yet there is the sound of the rapids loud to the left now, as we walk up the hill and that smell of the balsams, sweet and full. All over the air the perfect freshness of the balsam's smell. André ran up here with the canoe as if he were in a race. At least he is in good shape for what he has to do.

At the landing he stands in the sun ahead of us with the canoe near the short path to the river. Car in the shade will be cool. Not hit by the sun yet. André standing by the canoe tall as a tree from this angle. Walks down the path to the shore. Where I put in. "Did you put in here, Harry?" Take off my load and go down to join him. Watch the river sliding.

"Yes."

"And you went all the way? Over the falls?"

"Yes."

André back up to the canoe, carrying it down onehanded. Drops it in the water, holding the bowline. Get in. What are you saying to me owlbeard? Complicit smile up at me.

He hears that rapids all right. In the stern looking up at me. And not a word.

Say something Harry. Say it. "Comme je descendais des fleuves impassibles."

And smiling. "That's right. Come on Harry. Let's try it. One more time. Allez-go." Into the bow. Both holding on.

Janine running down to the edge. Shove off quick. "What are you doing André, Harry?" Turn and wave to her, now going, going fast. Into the fast water now, bouncing into the rapids, roaring, and listen André, the falls ahead.

the
lonely
ones

Montreal

Dizzying great towers all about me as I walk scot-free across this amazing big plaza or whatever. Wonder what day it is. Feels like they have just announced the first performance of The Bomb right here. Footfaults echoing in this vast and vaulty chamber seamed with the greed of a thousand eyes. Are you sure this is Montreal? With all these lonely great buildings about? Not like the campus I used to know from the dear old days. By God, the old fraternity house. With my seabag and secret grip. What an excellent thought.

Now this is better. Up this familiar old row of greystones the other side of the rather affected and dear old gates. Yes. McGill ever dear. No. Toronto is ever dear. What is John McGill, James McGill, something we see you standing there in your bright red underwear. And yes, the girls, the football, the excitement and all is for the best in this best of all possible worlds. Yes. My own small past gradually being cremated in this terrible present. No. I can't go back in there. I rejected the womb. But I could probably just visit for a while, languish, while I think over some important things. The house and the door. The secret Greek on the stone. Dully polished. Inside. The remembered odd long alley of stairs up the right, and the echoing vestibule, and the red tile dining room. Weird vaulty CPRchitecture of this union station interior.

"Hello sir. May I help you?" Smooth-faced young bastard calling me sir.

"Yes, by God, you can. Stop calling me sir."

"I'm sorry . . . What seems to be your problem?"

"That's better. A little due hostility. Proper snobbery."

"What?"

"I'm brother Summers. Toronto '65." The grip. Jesus. Am I doing it right? There. Up the wrist slightly with the. His frozen smile. Did I boob it? "There's nobody here just now. I'm running the house for the summer." He thinks I'm phoney.

"Yes, well, I'll just use Gaunt's old room for a week or so. My bags are following. Just back from the mouth of the Mackenzie. Geological." Jesus what if old Magee sold me the wrong grip. And I gave him the last of the bottle for it. Must face it out arrogantly going up these stairs expecting him to shout any moment.

"Now where is it again. Yes, here we are. Here's where Gaunt laid Peggy Sanderson. Out cold with a beertini. Do you still make them here?" to the footfaults behind me and this rather suspicious young man now quite unsure about me.

"When does school open again?" At least I remember enough to call it school. Yes. A simple B.A. Torontonensis teaches a lot of things.

"September."

"I know that, nit. When is September? How soon?"

"Couple of months, sir."

"Brother Summers, brother."

"I'm not a member, sir."

"You mean brother. And stop calling me sir. How come you're running the show if you don't belong?"

"I'm a Zate from Toronto." And oh the satisfied way he says that standing with his Rosedale English snobbery sticking out all over his smooth blond face and reddish healthy football cheeks. Or am I imagining it and he is actually just a nice kid trying to get by.

"What's your name, Zate?"

"Don Kelk."

"How do you do Don." Offering the hand again.

"If you thought I was a DU, Mr. Summers, why did you give me the Zate grip?" Not shaking. The overhead light falling like snow on his blondness. Snow on his shoulders. Offer to paint him and he calls me a fruit.

"Just testing you boy. Can't trust anyone these days. Now if you'll excuse me I'll just unpack."

"The room is twenty dollars a month. No meals."

"Okay. Here's the first month." Bloody pink money belt. Most awkward. "Where's the phone?"

Silently indicating the wall phone in front of me. Numbers of girls scribbled all round it.

"Thank you." And now to call Mike. André. Any girls I know here?

And my first love letter to Shirley.

> Dear Shirl,
>
> I write this on a lonely bed somewhere in Montreal pursued by the police of seven nations. At last my persecution complex has some reliable evidence to muster. I was today refused a card by the Montreal public library, and they could give me no valid reason beyond my thieving ways. The wedding presents are safe in my money belt. More than enough left to bring you over here.
>
> I wish I could do confession, but I suddenly feel incorrigible, rhymes with dirigible. Shirley, I feel tremendously free. I know that sounds awful, but there it is. At last free, you don't know what it means after all those years cribbed in England.
>
> I have just arrived after a longish trip, and am to

look up André here tomorrow. He is on some sort of Quebec nationalist kick which intrigues me. Revival of the French in me. Something is happening here in dear old Grannyda which I don't understand yet but which is mysteriously part of me. Anyway I DON'T feel chased and hemmed here, and I have for years thought I would. Rather the reverse, liberated. I was up at Lac Diamant last week with André and Janine. How you would like it if we could get you over here. Away from Them.

Now, I fear to tell you how much I miss you. I fear not because it is too late, the other way in fact – but because I will subside into the St. Lawrence for loneliness. You said you would come anywhere – will you come here? I shall be settled shortly, I believe. You will love it. Everything here suddenly seems possible again. Canada after Europe is like hearing Beethoven after Brahms. The fist up, the heart thumping, hope and struggle again.

How can I apologize to everyone? It is impossible. Just say I present my compliments, tell your father the bags fit fine and we are not all wild colonial boys. He'll remember Beaverbrook and Bernie Braden and all like that.

Write me please care of here and I send you love and kisses and an Air Canada ticket as soon as I find the office.

Please don't hate me. I do love you.

Love, H.

A bright and soulful morning. To the washroom and wetly scrape. Settle into this new life. See André first. Yes

Into the bright morning and all the way to the east end of this poor island. And up his stairs chuff. Why does André always live up stairs.

"André."

Whirls on me like a caught dog.

"My God, you scared me, Harry. Come in. Close the door. Is somebody there?" André wearing this apron bending over a strange machine.

"What's this thing, André?"

"It's the press."

And him feeling how he has excluded me from his confidence. "We had to go up and get it last week after the meeting. I didn't know where you were."

"Things are moving fast."

"Harry, last night they blew up a radio station owned by the Anglos in Chicoutimi. Somebody was hurt. I am in pretty deep. It would be dangerous for you to be involved here."

"Who blew up a radio station?"

"This bunch I am associated with. I cannot tell you their names. Please, have you got a cigarette?"

Triumph of producing a blue pack of Gauloises for him which he does not even remark.

"Thank you." Terrible lung-burning inhalation. Pointing it round the room. "This is a proofing machine. Stolen from Radio Canada printing office. Theft, burglary, sedition, inciting to violence, subversion, communism – I am in it to my neck." Suddenly stops and watching me slowly says: "Would you like to live here?" Huge laugh bursting like a zeppelin. Leans against map on wall resounding with laughs.

"Harry. What do you say? You are running away too, eh? Shall I report you to the police now? Have some good Bordeaux." And swigs from the bottle. Over to me. A short winey pull watching him.

"Are you painting here or what?"

"No. I'm in a Separatist unit. They are after me as well, Harry. And I look at you, running away too. What are we running from, eh?"

"Goddamnit André, you've had one-man shows. You won at the Biennale."

"Painting!" Up the bottle again and rolling his tongue through it. "Look, it is serious, very very serious. I am in it up to my neck. I'm afraid they will find me here if I keep coming round. I must move out, only come here to print."

"Print what?"

"These." Cheap pink stock breaking in your hand almost as you hold it. "FLQ" hastily done. "Quand les libertés sont mortes . . . aux étudiants de l'Université de Montréal . . . Que fait le FLQ? . . ." What indeed? ". . . vise à créer sur l'ensemble du territoire national un parti puissant . . . la clandestinaté, l'agitation et la propagande . . . l'indépendance ou la mort . . . message distribué par Le Reseau Duquette (1) Joseph Duquette, étudiant en droit, fut pendu en décembre 1838, à l'âge de 21 ans. . . ."

"Is this what you print here?"

"Yes. And at the cabin." Watching me for Anglo reactions now.

"Wow. Zut. Merde."

"They would like to wipe this out."

"Why did you do such a terrible job on the lettering?"

"Where?"

"This FLQ looks like a scrawl by a cretin."

"They just gave me the maquette."

"If you need me, I'm happy to come. But I don't want to get blown up. You know, I'm still a virgin. I want to find out what it's like before I let the worms in."

"I approve your recurrent virginity, Harry. May you lose it many times again. But it would help me to have someone here, a front for the front."

"Well, sure."

"You see, I could visit just to work the machine. You would never be suspected. It would be a free studio for you. I got it in all innocence as a studio. And I told you my way was paid back by the Canada Council? Yes. Fantastic, the resources that this sort of thing brings out in you. But this is paid for by my friends. I am supposed to open in Montreal next month, and all I have are the oils from Paris and Trouay. Nothing. I should have worked up plenty more by now. I can do nothing. Absolutely nothing. While I am in this condition. You're sure you want to live here? It may turn out to be dangerous. I ask you as a friend, after all. And I don't give a damn what Langevin says."

This means a great deal to him. I need a studio.

"Yes of course." What am I doing? "Of course André." And it is settled.

"Come for a walk." Down his stairs. How he pauses at the foot and leans his long body absurdly out. Looks up and down the street. Back in like a heron's neck.

"Look out there. Was that man there when you came?"

Derelict standing at the corner of ruins in this dusty east end with little houses wearing Pepsi signs hovering above him in the hot afternoon dustlight. Grey and blue-grey. Scene to. . . . "No. I don't think so."

"Okay. Out then." His long stride now curiously decelerated as we walk along the edge of this grey ruin that once held houses. This once-street rulering through the rubble piles.

"You are standing on lives." André high on a former doorstep to me walking towards him. "People's lives, French and Irish. Poor. You see what is left. This is how they lived, eh?"

Jacques Cartier bridge rising behind this, weaving wavering roadbed rising uncertainly, lumps of trucks grinding slowly up to the first arch all green rising to its foxy ears listening to all our complaints.

"Papineau's house over there," André pointing. "Monument to the dead patriots of 1838 and 1839 over there. Killed by the damned English. Hanged. Duquette. Corner of Papineau and Dorchester, right there. A bit of symbolism, eh?" As they intersect in a dry waste covered with old resentments. A touch of humility before his obvious sadness. "A couple of blocks over there, Joe Beef's tavern. My father used to eat there. And drink. You could get breakfast for five cents. What they called steak for ten cents. Miles of little row houses here, dirty and old and religious. At Joe Beef's they had two bears they fed on scraps. Now it is all wiped out so Radio Canada can have studios to assure us we are still vendus.

Vingt deux. I like the corner of Papineau and Dorchester. Tells me all I need to know about this country."

Silence. Men wrecking houses all around. Over to the east and lit with bright edges from the sun, stands a giant crane with little men on it. A dot swings onto a wall which crumbles obscenely. The men move as if rejoicing. They have lived there. We walk up and down over grey rubble like Back's men over the polar ice. We stop on a hummock of rubble undoubtedly over rats and feel the earth swaying under us. The unforgiving sun while André talks. Love death and revolution. Janine of the long face and complexion on the edge of giving up, who believes all and trusts all and suffers all. Lovely Janine who is so pure and so conscious of her body. Her green eyes are slightly aslant not quite matched in her pale and roselike face. Janine who I swear responds to me. Hush, concentrate, André is talking rapidly.

Painted green staircase unfairly exposed climbing stairless up a wall now toppling with a heavy rush onto the ruins of the house before. Watching it happen with my eyes unseeing staring like the psycho-neurotic that I am. Now strangely clear through my non-comprehension sightlessly staring, hearing André. He is fighting this, nothing else, the unfairness of life. Me too. With him.

"And I am sick of it, Harry, sick of it. We are all sick of it. In bondage to the owners, you and the Americans, and even our own kind. So I have to fight. You see, I have sold one of my favourite works to a great collector here. I didn't want to sell it but I was broke, and he had money. Now I know I can never get it back even if I pay the price he wants."

"Why not?"

"It is part of a deal you see, so I am out. Mr. Moore, and his kind, who own this world and sell it not for profit alone, but as they choose, part of a deal. Part of his priceless collection of Canadian art bought at low prices while the artists could scarcely sell enough to pay for the milk. That is the first thing I want you to do."

"What?"

"Come with me to see this man."

"All right. But what can I do?"

"Help me. He is an Anglo in Westmount, you see."

"All right. If it will help you."

"But it is his kind who have it all, Harry, all over. The control is with them, and it does not belong, it belongs to everyone. I was in bondage to him when I sold that painting, and I didn't know it at the time. Now I see the whole province is like that, in bondage, but it does not understand. So I have to fight it the only way I know how."

"So am I."

"You are? How?"

"Coming here, partly."

"You mean by running away."

"Maybe I've stopped running. For a while."

And his thinking look at me. "This is the place to stop. Right here, right now. This is the real struggle."

"I came across some huge square downtown the other day. I never felt anything like it in my life. It was inhuman. I thought the rockets were launched and everyone was hiding. Empty and nobody in the windows."

"Here is the beginning of the last struggle."

Beside me on this length of concrete atop the litter of bricks in the graveyard of houses where they are building.

"Where have all the people gone?"

"East. Making new slums. French slums."

Now walking one-foot carefully from broken block to block. The child's house has tumbled down. Talking as we go, back and forth now close now far as if a rubber band between us. The only fight I know. Domination of the Anglos. The bully Kirkpatrick at school that day, and me pulling him off and winning in the crowd on the cement yard. How good to stop the bully. Yes. Everywhere we are beaten down, the poor, the diseased, the minority that I am. But for once a champion in me with strength. Yes André, a man to follow through rubble, through this. And yes to him and yes to his fight. By god the moneygrubbers have had enough of us. The haters and bigots among us. Fight them. Beat them. Set up the new earth. Oh yes God that is a charge to lead. Do I hear you leading me? Is that a strange silence coming from you over this grave-yard talked through by unending André? Or the echo of my long day's indifference to you? No more. Committed to the good side.

"André. Stop. I have to paint this place." Shouting at him too far ahead. Him waiting on the former corner of the former street where are no more children playing. Coming up to him and the strange feeling of expecting him to grow proportion-ately larger as I close the last yards, but I am as tall as he is standing here.

"Look, I am with you. I will do whatever you need. Let me come here to paint first. I must sketch it." Low light, the jumble. It is perfect. "I see people in these stones."

"Come back to the studio first. I must show you some things."

"What?"

"Some books."

My *Refus*. My *Métier de Crève Faim*. My *Ligne du Risque*. Each on the other. *Parti Pris*. Issues and books and pamphlets atop each other like school days. "Christ, I don't need to read these."

Smiling at me. "I feel it may be useless, seeing you with all this. Is it too late for you? There are no converts to Israel."

"No."

"You know that."

"Not yet. Maybe." But I remember in Trouay, the day we talked. "Remember when we went on the bicycles down to the river at Trouay?"

"Yes."

"You say there are no converts, but that day, it seemed, not so. It was amazing how much we shared."

"I don't remember. You were so full of Shirley then."

"No, but we talked. We were homesick. We were trying to

get back over the sea again and see this country. The voices talking on the long sidewalks at night under the trees, the village going to church in the morning and hearing the bells ringing and listening to the terrible sermons and the protest in our minds against the tiny thoughts and all the hatreds of this huge country. We said we would bring out our new ideas and make them work, and put the old ones away like shrunken heads. Yes, I did and so did you."

"Yes. I remember that – Look, read these. You know *Refus Global*. Read the rest. You will understand. I must go for sure now. I have to meet someone."

"But André. . . ."

"It's late. I can't stop. We are all committed." And the look that refuses to talk.

"André, I have to know . . . is Janine living here?"

"No." Waiting at the head of the doorstairs. "She has – she is living at her sister's. The address is in the book there, by the phone. I've got to go."

"What happened?"

"Ask her. Goodbye. Leave this door locked, eh? I have a key here too."

"But you need to give me one."

"Here." Back in with one from his pocket. And gone like the answer in an exam.

The Studio

Blanking out in this narrow painter's bed with the cruel white light bouncing the propaganda facts from the cheap pages up at me. The very yellow thinness of the page bespeaking the agony of their struggle. Their old Canadian struggle to survive against us. How strange to see ourselves as selfish overbearing rogues from the other side of these similar words. Pierre Vadeboncoeur crying out against our North American presence and not even mentioning our name. As if we had never existed. Borduas against the world in a taxi driven by a starving man. To hang up your identity on the white man's hook every morning when you go in to work against your own survival.

Is he right? Do I owe it to him? The great North American sonofabitch whom we have both been fighting with our pitiful brushes. The great God Was, holding my soul against the god of possibilities? How they all agree the possibilities are now all on their side. As the commies used to do, and now would blush to shame. But in my loyalty I owe more than lip service. Nothing is round me but the old decadence, worse this time because it is the middle-class vulgarity; the worst exploitation is the exploitation of all by all, which we have believed was OK because we are all convicted together. And so kill the different, kill the French, the poor, the artist, all the rotten minorities that disturb the system. But how can it be fought? It prevails. It is the great American sonofabitch, creeping lustfully across the border into the bed of the equally lusting Canadian. Do we stop it here in André's and my conjoined fight against the vulgar totality? But I am as incompetent to rebel as to succeed so far in life. And the manifestation here in Montreal, city of *Métier de Crève Faim* is in old Moore ruining André, is in the poor cabbie asking, respectfully, his past full of bishops and politicians and condescending ladies who have never been east of Bleury, "How would you like to drive a cab for fifty dollars a week because you couldn't speak Urdu in your own hometown, Sir?"

What can I do? Decide? Too hot tonight. Just a hard sheet and the window onto the night sounds. Listening to haul and drum in neither tongue.

Janine coming towards me with her arms out turning into Shirley. I am running. Down this slippery corridor unable to stop. Each head from the porthole beside me as I run along beside the ship keeping ahead of the waves trying to hear what they say over the roar of the waves into the Gulf of St. Lawrence grabbing onto the edge of Newfoundland turning into a cookie tilting me into the sea alone where I have always belonged with father sinking and swimming down to him where he sits at a coral table weaving long strands of beautiful hair into these words that swim by me slowly unable to talk. Only to read what he says unable to talk to him but he knows me. He knows me. And we cannot speak. Take hold of them and rise lightly to the surface again. Words with meaning bearing me up. Oh the release from death by this beautiful strand of meaning. How right he is. How good, how full of love to give me this rescuing strand. How I love him. My only father in heaven helping me with these comfortable words that do me good to breathe again and standing on the earth blessedly alive. Waking to remember them. Must remember them.

What were they. Take hold. Something like take hold, and gone. Sitting silently spinning at the sea bottom for me. Take hold. What did the words mean? What were they? All effort ceases to remember them but gets in the way. Nothing left but the blessed feeling of relief. My young father dead and wonderful to me. To love the war that killed him. How can André know without a dead father? How can he know?

Razzle and flash. This wet night when the streets are canals. The great gondolas hashing along. Oblivious people staring along the shopwalks under the banging signs. The girls in arms, the boys separate watching and laughing. Rainslick on the softly going cars making them tolerable. And in snow, covered and frosted and full of faces looking out into the piled night going to a party in laces and furs. Clean hands on the wheel and my youth again. Once too much to bear and now its overflow comes out slowly in a dry season such as this. Come home Shirley, come to this lovely country of my imagination and live with me here.

Bookstores, drugstores, cars people walking lightflash. Have I passed it again? Always passing things in the night. Do I speak French or English to this lady asking for directions. English. A friendly tongue. So much French in my mind I am translating to her vague face looking past me as she tells me to go back. Too much makeup lady. What's the use of trying so hard at our ages, eh?

"Thank you." Merci.

"Oh, it's no trouble. Goodnight."

"Goodnight." Déranger, bonsoir. A leaping frog I am now.

This alley of Stanley. The crude hotel there. Looks like a pickup pad. Can she live here? No. Even number west, and she must be over there. I don't know what I am going to do. I know what I am going to do. God help it happen. No longer give a damn riding upstairs. In this impossibly rich apartment minutes high in the silent elevator. Even with me in it, it is empty and the red rug goes rolling along. Just keeps rolling along to Janine's door where I am sick with hope. My heart is knocking at the door.

"Janine. Hello."

"Harry. What is it?"

"May I come in?"

"Of course." The door opening and in out of the rain.

"Are you in trouble?"

Scarcely able to look at her, or around this wide apartment.

"No." What to say now? "I keep turning up."

"It is a lovely surprise." Standing looking me over. Making me feel gauche. But a friendly smile. Other Man's wife.

"I thought perhaps you could tell me why I'm here." At least a laugh from her. "Janine. I'm sorry. I am lonely. I don't know what to do. I wanted to see you so I came."

"Of course. Please sit down." On a chair. Tense.

"Thank you." Hands before me and the weight of what we both do not know yet. "The fact is my life is in ruins. Beautiful pieces falling all round me. I need someone to talk to."

Her decent concern. Letting me go on. Walk around starting in on it. Babbling. About London and the mess. But not to the point. Tense. Can't get started. Onto the sofa and try to be still and say it right. Janine now sitting down with a friendly smile. Why am I so hung up? Worse than I thought. But our two weights together on the pillows. Stop and think. Death and the revolution. "This is a nice place."

"My sister's. On loan to me for a little while."

"I don't know what to say. When I left London I was sure it would only be a little while, then I would send for Shirley. Now weeks have gone by and I haven't done anything. I was sure I would have sent for her by now, but I just haven't done it. I can't bear to say anything direct to her. I keep writing encouraging letters, but I can't bring myself to get her over. Even assuming she would come now."

"Is it over with Shirley?"

"Is it over with André?" Flat and negative responses joining. We don't know. But I have not been letting myself think that, strangely, despite all my protestations, something was over that night when she couldn't come with me. "I need a woman to talk to, Janine. I hope you understand that. I wrote to her when I got here, I didn't send her a ticket, I could have, I put it off, I don't know why. I guess I felt I needed more time, but why?"

"You have doubts."

"Yes." It is said. And who hasn't. "I hardly remember what I said in my letter. It was weeks ago now, and I've been mooning about. I've hardly painted anything, and that's what I thought I came to do, get away and work. I'm hung. And I haven't heard from her. They've probably arrested my letter."

Smiling at each other and sympathizing across the gloom.

"Shall we get drunk and talk. Or am I presuming too much on your liquor? I've got money. I'll go out and get a bottle."

"Don't bother. Just start with some beer."

"I feel like beer. Best drink for a man in trouble." The business of getting the bottles from her fridge. Her plain blouse and black skirt. Just a ripple here and there. I don't know if I want her or not. Can we talk?

"Santé."

"Dust in your eyes." Able to relax and smile. And talk. London. Shirley weeping. My dreadfulness. And protecting Shirley as I say it. "It wasn't her fault. You know, Janine, she is very kind and nice. Amiable. But something was missing, I think, not from her but from my conception of her. Something I could not grasp about her, some absence, or unwillingness, some place in her I could not reach or touch or even understand as being there at all. It took me so long to realize that, going to France, and then coming here. I just don't know."

"Well, I think you treated her harshly. But perhaps she needed it. She has troubles, Harry, bad as yours."

"And you and André?"

"Yes. It was sort of like that for us. You see, I believed he was an artist. He wanted to paint, and he did paint. I did understand him. But when he wanted to come home, and to do this, I began to lose sight of him. So for me, it was not that I did not know any part of him, but that I did not know all of him, all of André. Suddenly he was gone, taken away by something outside us both. The whole time we were in Paris after Trouay last year, he was leaving me. Leaving my idea of him. He became a revolutionary, patriot, thinker, talker, and activist. A new man was born there which I could not understand, and he did not want me to understand. He has been shutting me out of his life for almost a year now. You know those things you wear – the shells? parkas? Well, he was like that. He seemed to go into his own pocket and turn around and be something quite different, in a moment, closed against me. Tight." Drinking her beer a little. Not greedily. "You know how we lived. We used to visit the galleries. In Europe we went so many places together." Putting down her glass and sitting back. Offhand way she has of sitting. And lets me entirely into her confidence, it seems. And she protects him as she talks, against the devastation of judgement. As I did Shirl. This is a kind of friendship we have already.

"So I decided to come away. I felt he would come back when he wanted me to share that life again, or some part of the new one. But I could not stand being so far away from him when we were so close."

"Exactly what I felt with Shirl, though she did not separate from me, from anything that had existed up to then. She just did not feel, as I thought I did feel, that sudden living together, you know, that change of atmosphere that I thought I felt after I first came close to her. After talking like this. You know, just easy. She was an easy person, but it was by assent rather than sharing." To drink some more. Another bottle. As we stand in the kitchen thinking together. Her sloppy shoving movements as she thinks of something else, distracted as I am distracted and not knowing the world around. Thoughtful look at the blank counter. Ridiculous.

"Not that I mean, Janine, that talking this way for us is a . . . well, you know, I mean, it seems to me that we are phenomenally alike. Not the problem. The talking even. But our attitude.

And we are both emotional and impulsive. We both go out, and we care, and no secrets, sort of thing." Beery speech.

"Yes," thoughtfully, as I would and do. Just the same way. Myself in female. Odd. "Here's to you, Janine, I am very impressed." With a gainsaying smile. Which she takes just right. Easily. But it means something to her. "Janine, this is lovely. Being able to talk." As we walk back to the living room as if the place were our own. Thinking as we go, talking.

"I had to leave him." With her back to me. Let her talk. Therapy for me too. But not compete our two miseries. Very nice.

"I started to almost hate him. His friends. You know what they go around saying, and their magazines. 'I write well when I write badly.' So they speak patois, argot, joual – I suspect they make half of it up. They are crazy. Like children playing a game, and they don't know the gun is loaded. Well, they will find out when the gun goes off and someone is killed."

"Janine, they know. They know." Leaning forward with the incongruous gold beer in the glass looming festering richly beside me proving our unfitness to discuss this subject. Two Nazis debating the Resistance on the Boulevard des Italiens, dixneufcentquarantequatre.

"Yes. They don't know. Not only treason and rebellion, which I don't care about. It is self-defeating." And now she comes alive from that droll face, thoughtful and pointed, showing her fox brain now. Going to the heart of this animal of thought she has cornered. How André must have hated to see her this way. "They won't know what to do even if they win. It will change nothing. We will still be alone. We will still be a little French island in this vast sea of you. We will still have our Negro kings and our bad teeth and our impossible finances and our churches and priests and all we will be able to say is that we made it ourselves. It is absurd. And they don't know how to bring it about, much less how to make it work if they achieve it."

"Achieve what? Laurentie? Québec Libre?"

"That's just it. They don't know themselves. Oh, they are so wrong, and they have to have our support. I thought they needed me, all of us, emotionally, but now I see they don't. This is their own poor foolish game, and they think that Ireland and Algeria are a model. It is too late for that. I used to think it was a great dream, but now I see what is happening to these men – they are turning violent out of frustration. They have tried to make a complete break with Canada and the Anglos and the Americans, and they have also broken with themselves. Don't argue with me about this, Harry. I know it. When men turn violent this way, it is because they know they cannot win, and if they know they cannot win, why do they not tell us, whom they ask for support? No. It is finished. And they talk of Paris. I know people in Paris, and I have asked them about us, and they sympathize for us, but when we separate, there will not be a sou for us, not a single sou that is not exactly like the money of you and the Americans, and yes of our own rich. Do you know what we will get from Paris when we go out? I will tell you – a couple of speeches, a cultural ambassador, some editorials in the papers saying it is marvellous and that all Frenchmen are brothers. Shit. Excuse me. But it is the truth. Now – I am sorry – I am talking like a witch. Poor Harry." Settling back casually. And suddenly quite still. How many moods she has. Fascinating.

"Well, I don't know what to say. André has told me some things, but I don't know what I feel about this."

"He hates me now."

"No. Janine, no. He doesn't."

Shrugging. "Doesn't matter. What would he see in me anyway? A skinny kid from the wrong end of the city. Full of a nun's thoughts and rebelling against them. The real problem of Quebec is that we are slaves. There is no progress here except by rebellion. Always some kind of rebellion. Y en a marre."

And able to drink her beer after that. Impressive. How she is able to talk thus without losing her appeal. But rather increase it. To go to bed with a mind as well as all the other. I believe she feels me behind all this, and does not need me now.

But there is something in her, something that always was. That the removal of André and Shirley has made possible for us.

How simple and joyful to talk no-holds through this long evening discovering. You know what I know and more. And I can help you say something, and we agree on it. It is between us. Yes, but the undergraduate philosophers drinking the night down and finding total solutions and joyful agreement at the bottom of the glass.

A moment at the door departing. When we will meet again. Gone easily into the night cheered and no longer lonely. As if it had not been a parting. Oh Janine you lovely help. I skip down the street for you.

Suddenly running drunk in this business district. Once again to have dared and won. Even Janine a friend at last after the absurd yearnings. Free and free. Skip. Skip higher and run down this street. Run. Back to McGill.

Of course, I am a hypocrite. What enjoys me is this sense of conquest without complication. Nevertheless, there was good in it. She is happier and so am I. And she is closer to . . . sadness.

I have left my Shirley. Left her absolutely. Now on University running back to the city. The wires. The little shops and old tired apartments and the buses running by in their fog of smoke carrying home their loads of briefmen. To their Shirleys. The ones they love and cling to. The homes they make. Sober thoughts. Shirley. Alone in London while the wires run overhead. I must call her from the back of the bus speeding home.

But off at the fraternity house for the canny check. Waste of a ticket to go this one block. Back up to the gates and past them to the stone row. My box assigned for the duration and an actual letter waiting. Oh jesus, camp with mail under the pine trees waiting for them to hand it down. Actually in my hand Shirl. England and the Queen ripped open. "Dear Harry." All the way back to the studio Dear Harrying. From Shirley. She does want me. I know she does. She couldn't be this way if not. But first this cool study with the door closed behind me onto André's scene and sit on the bed making sure.

Dear Harry,

What can I say? You write so strangely after so long, and so much has happened. Daddy has just told me about the engagement ring and I don't know what to say. Was that part of it all? I understand completely, but you must remember, he felt he was helping us both; or that he was helping you do the right thing. Now I can just hear you say, that's the point, Shirl. All I can reply is, that part is over.

I can't bore you with my little doings, and besides I'm afraid of your opinions about everything here. Write soon, try to tell me more. I still don't quite comprehend what you have been through. You know what I feel.

I miss you. I'm waiting to see you.

Shirley

P.S. Don't for heaven's sake take this in any kind of discouraging way, proving something disastrous. I'm afraid of what your momentary feelings will make you do. I miss you and I love you and I'm getting over that fantastic week. People are so solicitous when they see you in a situation they wouldn't like for themselves. Goodnight dear, love Shirl.

Passing. Over. It is going. Not too late. Best thing in my life, and not to let it go because of the damned circumstances, and her single cool fault of never being quite committed, or showing it to me, or whatever the hell. Write, Harry, write and pluck her from that fog. Get it back while you have time. The last-minute try at which you excel. Wham – over the top and life committed, last time. Write write write. All caution gone and tell the truth. Yes.

Dear Shirley, Shirley dear

I want you to come right away. I haven't got a proper room yet, but it should be easy to find. Can you get yourself ready to fly in a hurry? I have the money and

I shall buy the ticket here and you can pick it up there. I have it arranged with Air Canada.

This country is fantastic now. As soon as I can get a decent room, you will see it, and it is unbelievable. The feeling in the air is tremendous excitement. I am mixed up with André in a movement of tremendous social protest – that sounds so pompous for what it is, really changing a whole country from the youth up. Everything is young here, and I did not know how this could be, before now. Hope, creation, it is all wonderful. The galleries are full, the painting scene is fantastic, though I have scarcely worked, just walked around trying to get used to it, get it into me. The young people have taken over to a fantastic degree, literature, films, painting, everything. Of course, some of it is bad, but I have never felt so moved and changed in my whole life. I am only regretful it didn't happen to me before.

When I get things lined up I'll phone you.

I have to go see André now at the gallery, where he thinks I will be able to show. It is the best in the city, and he is introducing me to them. I think I can get a one-man in the fall, or at least, part of a group show. Then we're off to a meeting of his group, I think.

Love and love and mille tendresses.

Harry

Another lonely lunch in Joe Beef's. How many have I had. Thought they would be over with dear Shirley. Coffee in this thick mug. Now there's a pretty figure in her white waitress' costume with the thin strip of her pants showing below. Ahoy below. And see that figurehead. Wow. Ugh. But a dime to you all the same. To buy you a mask, honey. Up and down the arty sidestreets with my unmailed letter under oaks walking and looking into windows in old grey houses along these steep sidewalks to the mountain bright with oils and tapestries and wild sculptures standing weirdly outside assaulting the rectangles from which we build. The disgusting Prop art that afflicts the scene these days. Nothing in it. The hacking of the untalented against the dim body of their ennui. Look at that brazenly in the window. Squares bent by the ripple of myoptics. Marvel of fartheadedness. A giant soup label badly reproduced in bad taste. To pin new pop art to a board and sell it. Here is what you wiped yourself with this morning, sir. Five hundred more of the same please.

Decide, Harry, decide. Mail the letter after your fit of enthusiasm last night. Then to face André's kind and frightening invitation. Face Shirley. Face your painting career in which you have been forced to half disbelieve all the time, as with Shirl. And now do it.

Tuck it in the box. How simple once it is gone. To sit here waiting till the mailman comes so I can get it back. No, get away before the bloody thing blows up. I wonder if they put the bombs in because the Queen is on the box, or because the mail service is terrible. Anyway, we're off to see the wizard at his wonderful gallery not far from somewhere around here. Yes, there it is, Galerie Lefebvre, and along this famous old street to its undoubted eminence, trying to sell André Riancourt to these rich masses. Up the stairs and into the good old smell again.

But there is André standing with the owner. Let them talk privately while I walk round looking at what is happening here these days. Op as it can be. Most ocular painting the world has ever known. All for the iris. A good thing, where no mind matter is involved. Involved. Jesus, André has seen me. Now I shall have to meet that nice lady owner and confess he is only being nice to me.

"Harry," and how appropriate he looks today in black sweater and cords and brown desert boots. I feel out of it bowing to this nice lady who obviously owns the world of painting in this city. Hardly able to look at her as I am being compared with this truly great man of Canadian painting beside me.

"Have you exhibited in Canada before, Mr. Summers? Do you have a dealer here?"

"No. Not in Canada."

"I see." Her blue eyes watching me to go on, but her kindly smile is wasted on me. I can scarcely look at her. Say something Harry, but I can't. Inferior.

Suddenly André is talking for me. Thank you, owlbeard. Yes, the show in London this winter, with Av. Red And Orange Affectionate sold to the Tate. Not bad that. But after that the English show where I was hung in Paris and not one sold. Two years ago. The honourable mention at Barcelona. He's got it all correct.

"Well, the judges were just being kind, I thought." A glance at her, who is not surprised. "I think they were so surprised to have an entry from Canada that they lost their heads."

"Will you be having a show this fall, Mr. Summers?" She is getting impatient now. Wants me to come on.

"Well, I don't know. I have no dealer." Shameful confession, paint five years and no dealer in your own home country.

"Could I see some of your work? Oils, drawings, acrylics? What do you work in?"

"Oh you know, everything. I did some intaglio drawings in London I could show you. I haven't any oils here just now."

"I see. Well, I'd be very glad to come round to the studio if you would give me a call. Perhaps we could arrange something for late this winter, if all goes well."

"Oh yes, I'd like that. Very much." And for the first time I can look at her and smile. And I do see some pain lines in your face, lady, so it's okay. And away she walks leaving us here. Stay André stay where my shame is smeared all over. I can stand in this pool of fear and inferiority with you to save me from it.

"Let's have a beer."

Turning to go with him. Look at your shoes.

"André, I'm sorry." Mumble to him as we go down the long front steps.

"What's wrong?"

"I was no good, I was terrible. What could I say?"

"Well, it doesn't matter. Come on." And along the street to wrap our fist around a cold glass in the outdoors looking back up to McGill.

"Didn't you like her?"

"I hardly saw her." A long swallow. That's better. "I was scared, that's all."

"But why?"

"Do you think I am an artist. Soap box labels, a couple of little shows. One major sale. One, in my life, and no major prizes. And I have to go in there and face her. She's the best dealer in Canada."

"Oh there are lots. All you need is confidence."

"Thanks. I mean it. Thank you." And now so shy at the dean that I do not feel it is right to sit at his table. André, you did me a great honour taking me in there. I couldn't have gone alone. Not a single oil to show. I came away too fast. Some drawings. What's . . . this? Oh." Pulling out the Rosenthal clipping from *The Listener*. "Hah. My only good review, and I forgot to show it to her. I even brought it." Handing it to his outstretched and prizewinning hand. He reads.

"Very nice. Very respectful and enthusiastic. A very good combination."

"Thanks. You did all the talking for me. I . . . well." What to say. Him waiting decently. A friendly smile. "Really, you were damn decent, and I'm grateful. I'm buying."

"Okay. But you weren't talking so I had to. Now look, if you're too nervous to come along with me, just say so."

"Never. I'll go beard the great Moore with you." André's hopeless quest to get a painting back now that his price is so high. Oh well. With him. Blinded by this city sun watching the summer moving alive along Sherbrooke Street.

"Let's go." And to walk along the street here having paid for him and being accepted here as well by André. How pleasant to be home this summer in Montreal. Maybe I am at last living. Long André seems to know so many people about here. Stopping everywhere as we go to say hello, French or

English, to wave to someone along the street. People saying how glad they are to see him.

"André, this street is like your salon."

"Very good." Walking a little away from me, perhaps distracted by all this hominess. Looking confidently back at me. "Come on Harry, keep it up, it's just up on top of the mountain there. I'll run with you."

And suddenly here we go up Mountain along the street towards Westmount laughing and running out of breath. Shirt flap and footpounds, but don't let him get ahead. Even. Ahead. Even. He's slowing. Thank God. Bending over hands to knees. Look at him leaning against the stone wall going up the steps ever higher.

"This is a fine . . ." him trying to breathe ". . . way to arrive in Westmount, eh Harry. Running. It is forbidden to move faster than a baby carriage here."

"You call that running. Hell, where I come from, that's no faster than a kid going to school."

"Oho, you want some more. Okay." And here we go again, running, stopping, running, and at last walking entirely out of breath unable to talk but saunter under the great old oaks and maples of this famous place. Higher and higher we go in the afternoon until we can see the whole city spread out to the riverline far off, square-topped houses retreating down the mountain in awe of this citadel, down to the docks and highways. And the far plains stretching to the south hot and blue and grainy with the distance.

"This is Westmount, André?"

"Citadel of fine old collectors. Fortress of the mighty."

"I've never been here before. It looks very posh."

"Symbol of hated domination. Look, see the defiant Union Jack." And there it redly flies, all angles and stripes, hung from a stone house in honour of some distant British occasion. Green lawns and flowers. A Rolls every now and again, and nobody walking but us intruders. No children playing. Just huge houses abandoned for the summer while everyone goes to the lake.

"A nice life. South in the winter, and north in the summer. Does anyone live here? How do you know Moore will be home?"

"I called. Here we are."

And up the long walk past a lawn cut today yet without a blade of grass on the stone walk. Shadows of the trees lying cool on the walk and cool on the stone wall. Peaceful and beautiful. Soundless ring within as André pushes the gold button by the yellow oak door. Mr. Moore, round and red, at the door to welcome us. The cool gloom within on his pink fresh cheek. Shaking his cool hand with mine new oiled from running here. Down a long Persian runner past oak panelling to the gallery at the back. Incongruous but marvellous a huge billiard table in the centre of this monster room and all round, Riopelle, Letendre, Chagall, Sutherland. Mr. Moore oh perfect small and round and pink and white and smiling in a blue pin-stripe suit welcoming us with scotch and soda in the brilliant day.

"Thank you." Crystal deep square tumbler.

"I must compliment you on the collection, Mr. Moore. It's beautiful just to stand here." Not to gauchely put my drink on the green felt. But hang on to it though it is so heavy. His curiously high voice with the soft A's coming to us.

"I'm glad you're back, Mr. Riancourt. It will be nice to walk into a gallery of your work again."

"I haven't done much recently. But I have plans."

"I'm sure. I have seen reproductions of what you showed in Paris last year, some transparencies that Madame Lefebvre brought back. I was impressed. Enormously impressed."

"Well, good." But he is looking around now, for that painting. *La Femme de Beauce*.

"I have been wondering when I would have the chance to view some more of your work."

"Well, yes, soon I hope." And Moore turning to me now asking politely about mine. Nothing to say to this rich collector. Still polite, but he is getting a bit puzzled. Tell him André, tell him. Now he starts.

73

"I don't see that, do you remember it, I wonder. A small painting I did some years ago. It was the head of a girl from Beauce. I was still doing figurative work then, do you remember it, by any chance?"

"I think I do. Standing by a house, looking over some fields."

"Yes, that's the one."

"I remember, yes, you were doing something odd with the fields and forests in the distance then. You developed that, refined it, later on. Deep patterns, I remember. In blues and golds."

"Yes."

"I am not sure where it is. Will you excuse me? I'm alone at home, the children are away with Mrs. Moore at Magog. Let's just go in and see if it's here." And he turns on a light into the living room. Paintings everywhere. Incredible. André longlegging up to the end of the room and back. Disappointment.

"I don't see it anywhere." Moore standing thinking.

"I sent some back for reframing. Mrs. Moore thought the frames were too heavy. But no, it wasn't in that batch. No, I think it was sold. Yes, now wait a minute. I'm trying to remember. I gave some paintings to the Beaux Arts. Was it with them? Yes, now I remember, it is with a dealer downtown, who is sending it to Toronto. A collector there was interested in some paintings of the Montreal school, and he was going to buy half a dozen."

"Oh. Is it sold then?"

"I think it is."

"I see."

"I'm sorry. If I had known, I would certainly have kept it for you."

"Do you remember the name of the dealer?"

"Yes, here I'll write it for you." And taking a thin gold pen from his weskit pocket. Dangling fraternity pin on the gold watch chain. Carefully inscribing André's fate on a slip of paper from his pocket notepad.

"Do you remember how much he was paying Mr. Moore?" My voice suddenly shattering this polite calm.

"I'm sorry, I can't remember the exact sum."

"It might be possible for André to get it separately, you see."

"Yes, well, I'm afraid if I remember it correctly, the deal has gone through, and it was part of the whole package."

André glancing at me to take it easy.

"Excuse me for interrupting." I must take it easy. "I just know how much it meant to André. Perhaps I needn't explain to you what a certain painting will mean to someone, how he sees it as part of his life. If anything could be done . . . ." Shut up Harry, you're making it worse. But poor André over there looking so crestfallen and hopeful.

How I felt after selling that crazy one all the corners driving into the centre and masses of feeling in it, dimension of paint, and how I know he wants this one back. "If it is a question of money, Mr. Moore." Suddenly feeling rich with this money belt close here full of hundreds. "I could maybe help you out. He doesn't want to make a profit on it, Mr. Moore. He wants to keep it."

"Well, I couldn't embarrass Mr. Riancourt with . . . I mean, the whole thing is concluded. I'm very sorry. If I could do anything. . . ." Sitting forward round and small on his deep soft chair looking pained. André with his head down shrugging. Never mind, never mind. Silence. Say no more Harry. Wait.

"Would you like another drink?"

"No thank you. I guess we. . . ." André getting up.

Walking away. Down the hall. Goodbye stiffly at the door. Down the walk. Is the door closed behind us? I ruined it.

"Thanks for trying Harry."

"I'm sorry I said that about the profit."

"You should have. You should have asked him how much he made on his package deal of the Montreal school. He's probably sold it for five times what he paid."

"It didn't seem to reach him. The bastard wouldn't even call the dealer."

"He was lying. He knows perfectly well the deal has gone through. He knows every painting he ever bought or sold. He trades in them. He's damned good at it."

"Goddamn pool table. You know how they light those things. Did you see the spots over the table. What the hell. You can't see paintings that way. It's a bloody crime."

"Well Harry, how do you like our colonial status, eh?"

"I could tear his pinstriped lapels off and beat him to oblivion."

Laughter from André. "And are you bitter, André?"

"You see, I'm bitter because he gives me nothing to be bitter about. There is the heart of what I feel – rich man buys us, and when you are bought suddenly the price goes up and you can't buy yourself back. Do you see it now, eh Harry? The whole goddamned province is sold out. What Duplessis didn't sell, we sold individually. And goddamned Moore, how can I object? Why do you think I was so quiet in there? He bought me early, when no one else was buying, he paid a fair enough price. But I know goddamned well he could have got that painting back for me now, and given it back to me, for the money he has made on me for my other work. One little painting is all I want. Just one back out of the eighteen he has bought, and he says awfully polite, no. Do you wonder how I hate this goddamned system when I see how it enslaves us. If you're poor, you have to sell, at their price, and so you stay poor. And if you go away as I did, and do something about it where it counts, abroad, and you come back, you still can't buy back your heritage. So the hell with it. Blow it to hell." To walk along hating the power around us. With its air of legitimacy. Its semblance of legitimacy.

"A deal is a deal André, isn't that it? Especially if it is to the other guy's advantage."

"But what I detest," his anger, slamming his hand on his fist, "what I despise, is that I would have paid his price, I would have paid what he wanted from that dealer, but it was a package deal on the Montreal school, he'd done a good bit of business, and he didn't give a damn about me, Harry, not a damn about the man who painted the work. Jesus."

"I know, I know. Never mind. Calm down."

"I know." Not looking at me but away and slowing down, stopping. "But I knew all that when I went, I wanted that confirmation, I wanted to test what I suspected. And now I know. I had almost no hope when I went. But I wanted to see him, I wanted – oh I don't know – to come up against him, you know. You see, I used to feel something for him, years ago. He encouraged me, and now I have no illusions about why. I am part of a package deal of the Montreal painters, and that is that. I can say shit to the Moores of this world, I owe you nothing, you see, because you made a profit on me, and I am free of your patronage. You are paid off. Now let me go."

The air is as bright as it was. But it is now purely visual. Unpaintable, unfeelable. Back downtown for another one, and then to sit like a couple of absinthe drinkers thinking about the fate of the buggered artist. Ruined by society and left to bear the shame of it. "But I must not be too cynical. It can't be that bad."

"Not everywhere. Not always. When you get the chance to put up your price fifty per cent, put it up one hundred. Get what you can. Life is long and art is short."

"Yeah."

"Where are you going now?"

"The studio."

"Okay, I'll see you there on Friday. Afternoon. Keep painting."

"I will. And thanks for the introduction to Madame Lefebvre."

"It was nothing. Goodbye."

"Au revoir, André. Don't let it get you down."

"Oh, hell. It's nothing." And off leaving me with a handful of foam. One more and back to the tired building. Plan a painting if I have the energy. When do I ever plan anything?

And back home here slept out. To look out his good big window to find out what day is it? Today, naturellement. Breakfast of bananas, peanuts and milk. The artful starver. A man can live years on that diet for about twenty cents a day. As long as he doesn't go crazy.

Now no longer avoiding it today. What I was after yesterday. Encouraged to paint by that distant promise of a show. Yet what I did yesterday was yesterday's greatness, and today it doesn't look so great.

Measuring myself against his talent. His dozens of canvasses stacked against the walls. His pinned-up parody of Leonardo's faggy horses, and the missing space on the wall between Leonardo and Picasso's horses which he has filled for fun with the French milk dray coming down a blue street at morning. The proofing press with its awful load of pink paper yellow paper cheaply arrayed looking ready to break at the first run-through. The dim smell of his oils and portrait after portrait of Janine in the thousand moods, all charcoal. How he has hated to work any of them up. This man's life has come to a complete halt while he changes a tire. The sonofabitch politicians, they should not be so bad that the innocents have to go in and ruin themselves where they are not acquainted. All as I work.

I am apprentice to this suddenly enfeebled brush. Another short rest, and then to work. A little lie-down here.

"When Coleridge woke up, he had a poem of genius. All you have is a hardon."

"Jesus, you walk around with that great knob ringing in your pants like the clapper of the Liberty Bell. How are you?"

"Come here, let me show you this." And he walks to the easel that I have been afraid to uncover. "Here's what I was working on when I left. I wanted to work today."

On with the light.

"Stage one. Look." Off the brown paper and this gleaming

beauty under. White paint all over. The raised lines indigenous in that environment. Christ, what an excitement here. He is so great.

"Look, you see what I've been working on. It's marvellous. I do the design on paper first, just play around. It works out by itself, then I transfer it to canvas. I slash the canvas very carefully with the blade – let me show you" and how he works silently now with tremendous speed – God, how I have always liked his speed and care paired. Low light low sky landscape conventional shapes and in the brilliant water, the design, cut, angled, mostly straight lines but very thoughtful – a very thoughtful painter he is – and just slit the surface of the canvas gently, yes so, like that. Watching his large hands with care go surely over the innocence. Now for the all over white. Yes. Good texture. Design to be brought through the later paint.

"Of course, the conception changes sometimes as I see the paint go on, but the idea is to bring the design through a perfect transparency of paint to the surface, just as it happens in water. You know how the appearance of a reflection on water is affected by that skin on still water, that overglow of the sky."

"Yes, yes."

"Well, I bring it through the paint just that way on canvas. I have to mix very carefully, use the colours very very carefully, like the melodic line in a symphony – all related and yet orchestrated, in one tone. Incredible effects. It is like painted thought, and yet it is totally visual. This is what I was working on in Paris. I am a good way along with it."

"Have you finished anything?"

"One, here, yes, see. Look at it. I want to call it something like lake of thought."

Conventional but meticulous distant shoreline. Deep deep water into which I see with all my mind. Huge masses of water perfectly designed, as if we see into the depths. Monotonous blue-grey tone. Deep pacific struggle of water.

"Drowned land. No, waterthought. Yes. Two visions. André, it is fine, very fine. Deep."

"Do you think it comes off?"

"Yes. I think you had some trouble here, eh?" The water under the far points that do not quite meet.

"Yes, at first." His long finger in a straight line rising and then shearing off to the right of the crisis in the painting. "I thought I had taken the balance over here. No?"

"Yes, but I can see it."

"Bastard. Yes, I know. But anyway, it is done. I had to shift it and I think it works."

"But it is good, André, very very good. I admire it."

Standing here before it looking at him. I am as tall as he. How did I not notice before? We are level. His smile on his wide mouth in the nest. And wide eyes alive. Him respecting my opinion. Winner at the Venice Biennale. One-man show last year with six sold in Paris. Now on the first team with him for a moment.

"I keep moving. I can't rest. This is completely new for me. Already I can feel a way to work on from this."

"I hope you will. But keep alive."

"Hey, should we go up north sketching again? I have to get back. Get in shape again. Do you know I can't paint when I'm out of shape? I have to breathe clean air. That's why I don't paint down here. Or in Paris."

"You painted that show all last winter in Paris."

Now putting the work carefully away. "I'm nervous about leaving them here. You will take care of them?"

"Sure André."

"I didn't really paint last winter. I just took the ideas that came to me in the country and worked them up. I had to walk four miles every day to keep up. I used to go through the Bois in an hour and have tea in the café at the far end. That's where I met Pierre. Where I decided to come home."

André over to the long bed and lying down. Nervously punching the pillow into shape. Long bones hanging over the bed's edge, big long hands playing back and forth with the brush. Painting on air.

"My heart goes out to you, you poor bleeding suffragette."

"I don't need your pity." Brush like a rifle now. "I will be out of this in six months and working like a madman."

"You know, I've been working towards this same sort of approach for a long time now."

"You are a funny guy, Harry, do you know?"

"Why do you say that?"

Annoying way he keeps looking at me through the sight on that rifle.

"You don't think about your work. You just slap it on any old way and there it is. Everything I do is planned. Very carefully."

"I paint from my heart."

"That's your trouble. Paint is in the eye. Painting is a matter of careful thought and swift execution. You don't concentrate."

"Yes I do."

"You paint from emotion. But this is a society of heads we live in. Everything is in the head now."

"Why are you on this emotional Québec Libre parade then?"

"Why? Because I am an emotional Frenchman too. I am overwhelmed by the despair of my people. Remember your quote from Picasso. The artist cannot live in an ivory indifference. Painting is just a means of carrying on the war on another front. But anyway we are different. I regard all the limitations of oil and canvas as opportunities. I think you do not."

"No, I exploit what there is."

"Well, a six-months' holiday for me, and we shall see."

Up and around. Impatient walk as if he did not like this mere earthbound locomotion. Suddenly stops.

"We are starting to play our little game with the radio station, Harry. Do you still want to play?"

"What do I do?"

"Drive the car for us, and take us inside. We are a folk-singing group, and you the rich English-Canadian impresario. Exploiter of the Pepsis."

"Impresario? One would suspect the clothes, instantly." Patting my unseemly threads. "Of hiding something?" Finally he laughs with me. Beautiful.

"A bomb maybe, Harry? What are you concealing in that marvellous toga of yours, eh? Photographs of a Turkish wedding?" Walking around me like a suspicious cop. "I would search you but I don't know the cure." Tapping me laughing. "How long have you been dead, my man? Eh? Have you a permit to offend the public dignity, eh? Now let's see, this bright red hairy English afghan coat with the foxhunting flap in the back and the plastic elbow pads falling off." Tearing one off and scrutinizing suspiciously twirling on the end of his brush. My pad.

"For leaning on maidens' thighs. There were complaints previously from the mothers that my elbows left dints."

"And these apparent pants are for crawling through sewers, evidently. Why have they this unusual décolletage in the front, eh? Are you some kind of show-off?"

"No sir, actually I pee out the back. This is just so I can get my money belt in a hurry."

"Ah, yes, your famous money belt, which I suspect is some kind of absurd girdle. Does it contain anything more than your disgusting paunch? And that shocking pink colour. Very Ontario, I assure you. I believe you are safe from any Mountie with that to prove your English ancestry. What can one say about these pants except zut. They look like Dali's wiping cloth. They bag like de Gaulle's eyes. Your shoes. A footnote in Krafft-Ebing. Fantastic. Green running shoes."

"I play on nothing but the finest imported en tout cas."

"Evidently, and very badly, to judge from your pigeon-toed stance. But the marvel is this mosaic shirt with the mosaic tie. Tell me, sir, how did you arrive at this elegance? Was it alcohol? Opium? Or charity? Hah hah."

"Will you just state the charges?"

"Certainly. An offence to the public eye. Impersonating a corpse."

"Guilty."

"Once more the puritanical Ontario conscience convicts you.

Charge sustained. Sentence: to paint a self-portrait after Buffet. Your brush sir." And handing me his brush like a rapier over the arm.

"From such a second I accept the comedy. And a pleasure to see you on the crest again, sir."

"I must go. Harry, once again it has been comical. We meet at Boulogne."

"What is the password?"

"Comme je descendais des fleuves impassibles."

"No, seriously."

"What for? Say you knew me at Maison du Québec. Am I a spy in my own country?"

"André, you silly bastard. You made all this up, not me. I'm just trying not to go wrong."

A hand round my shoulder. "You're right. It is serious. Very very serious. It is also full of schoolboys just out of lectures on Marx and Papineau and Aquin. Don't let the atmosphere infect you. In those clothes they would never believe you anyway. Come on."

What the hell is he up to? "Where are we going?"

"I'll tell you as we go." Walking beside this heron along the edge of wasteland. "We have a plan. We are to seize a radio station and broadcast a message."

"What kind of message?"

"Part of a bigger plan. Just a small part of a massive demonstration to awaken the people of this province. Well?"

"Well what?"

"Never mind." And walking away from me.

"André." But he is not stopping. Run after him. Stop him.

"What's the matter?"

"I thought you said at the studio you understood."

"Well, I did, I thought I did."

"Well then?"

"Well what? I'm listening to you."

"But you are not reacting. You don't care."

"I told you I cared."

"It's useless to discuss it if you don't care."

"André, you're being impossible."

"There is a meeting, I must go. I'm sorry."

"Well, I'm not finished. Why the hell should you run around doing this. You're a painter."

"Let me tell you one simple fact of life here. Our articles are refused by the press, partly French-Canadian capitalist conservatives and partly Anglos who own the magazines. The radio is controlled by the federal. And the television. There is no chance to make our views known. All right? do you understand that much? We have no press, no radio, no TV. So we can have no publicity and therefore no political action. Do you understand that as well? Superb."

"Oh cut the shit."

"All we can do is demonstrate for that right. That is what we propose. I ask you only to keep your mouth shut. Will you do that?"

"Goddamnit André. You don't have to ask that." Sad. André like this. What Janine must have been through.

"Harry. I'm sorry."

"You should be."

"It is very hard to understand. You see, you thought you did, and now you realize you did not. It is as simple as that. This is something that must be felt. We are trying to be free. If you do not feel oppressed you cannot want to free yourself. I can't make you feel what this is. I see now you do not. It's no use."

"I have tried to show that I do know, and I do understand, and that I do feel. I only ask that—oh hell André—what do you want me to do?"

"You say you care. Why?"

"Because you're talking about being free, and I believe in that."

Standing on a sidestreet with a verandah zooming over our heads trying to hear over Jacques Cartier twenty feet away.

"We go up this way." And he is leading me into it.

Three streets and corners past dusty barefoot children on cement. Where a truck and a car fill the street, house-wall to wall. Little front verandahs onto the dust and people sitting there, a man looking at us, a woman with a baby in her lap. Excuse us for walking past your lives. Now up a set of wooden steps and to a yellow front door freshly painted. In a narrow hall, Jean-Jacques greets André and does not look at me. Accepted. Linoleum endlessly down this clean hall, and into the right living room. Two young men. Jean-Jacques tall and rangy like André now shaking my hand and seeming nervous. Philippe and Langevin. Red-haired Langevin.

André explaining me. Others have apparently already agreed but red Langevin without looking at me expresses distrust in his face. My naïveté in thinking they needed me for any purpose other than because they are short of bodies. One to listen outside for something, three in the group of singers. Alouettes. And me to manage.

But first: "Will you have a cognac?" Jean-Jacques, thin and classical with the quick look. Radio man I bet.

"Yes. With a little water please."

His look. Passing them round eventually. Mine neat. And "Excuse me, I hate to put water in the cognac. Would you take this?" And André's laugh. At least a hand on my back. "Water puts out the fire, eh? Come on, Harry. Drink it." And watching me take it down. Quenching the last scruple. And over the plastic-topped and horrible table spreading out a map of the station grounds, parking lot, all to scale, and the plan of the building. Dates. Times. Me to drive the car and speak the English at the door. For August. Over a month.

Find out the type of machine they use and tape the message at the proper speed. Broadcast quality. Disguised as folk singers able to bring in a tape recorder. But that involves losing it there perhaps, and too expensive. But easy to rent one and leave it. I to lug it as the manager. A suit? And that's why he teased my rags.

"No, not here in Montreal."

"We'll lend you one. You must look the role. You do drive a car?"

"Yes. And I can speak English." Suspicious of my light

touch there. But this is all in the rapidest French and full of slang. Recap en français to make sure I have it all straight. They now listening intently. My slow words. Curiously clumsy just now with it.

"Speak English." André curt as to a dog.

"Il me faut d'abord comprendre en français. Le complot se déroule en français, il s'agit de . . ."

"D'accord. Excusez."

"Grazie."

And getting it all virtually right first time around. To drive the car to the parking lot at eight o'clock. Take them in past the doorman who may or may not be on duty then. Up to the second-floor broadcast booth and look lost. Then two men from the station in with us take over the booth and the master control room and we go on the air. If caught, we run, but there is no shooting. Only to set the tape going and guard the door till it is off the air. André to hold the walkie-talkie out the window to receive a message from Jean-Jacques in the car below listening to the car radio that the tape is okay. Then we go out.

"Yes. And don't forget the guitar cases. They have to have real guitars in them, and they are borrowed for the occasion. Expensive."

"Okay." All set. And now I can go. Like a child from class, as André takes me to the door.

But back to the room first to thank Jean-Jacques for the brandy. Host to a cell. "Good night."

"Good night and good luck. We'll be in touch with you."

André sees me to the door. Outside.

"Is there anything else to do before we go to the station?"

"No."

"Why is it not sooner?"

"Our contact man there has just been hired. He does not know all the routine and the equipment yet. We must give him time. Sit down."

To sit on the wood steps in the fashion.

"We'll go to the cabin right after. Use it now if you want."

"Okay. And thank you André. I would like to go away for a while, if I can manage it."

"Is there anything else?"

"I don't think so. We'll just talk at the studio again, eh mon général." No smile from him. "You are very serious, André."

"I am grateful Harry. Believe me. We needed you. Everyone says we are doing a foolish thing. One of the other people refused to come into our plan, and we are no longer part of the main movement."

"But why?"

"He thought we were becoming too independent. So it is just Langevin, Jacques, Philippe and myself." His blue-green eyes on me seriously out of his long worried face. "This must remain absolutely quiet. Forget everything but your own part, and tell nobody about it."

"Yes."

"Thank you." Get up and shake hands formally.

"Take care."

"And yourself."

Down the steps. Back along the street forgetting as I go except that middle-class living room with the red square chairs and plastic coffee table and the three earnest young men awaiting us. Sons of families. In their own living rooms and parents probably horrified. Cognac in the afternoon and Lenin. Am I a fool and curse? Or is this the only possible way? You have to help somehow. You have to help them.

Looks as old as Cambridge here and as vast: grey stone, copper green, beautiful old poor.

What I do not know about him, I do not know about myself: why. His friendship no longer reaches out to me. He uses me, and that is all. It is not him and me anymore. There must always be a third thing to bring us together, Janine, the revolution, the escape cabin, painting. Something. How did it happen?

Grey town, old houses, dead men and dreams. Christ what a rubble we live in. Dust all over our hopes, and the more prosperous we are, the more we want the revolution to save us.

It is not our apathy, no, our unthinking energy. The too many canvasses unthought and bought. I should think this?

Must work up a show. Must. Must. Can't get down to it walking along a narrow French street here with the dogs and cats in the summer eve. Can't get down to while Shirl Janine André. Bell clapper, you give precise and powerful information, and still something is missing. Something I can't see, can't figure out. Everything is between us that counts and I can't quite succeed to it. In the dark we reach out, we touch, we feel, we speak and what are we saying? I hear it, I say it and it is not there afterwards. And what is an instance of it? So wordy, say it so many times, have so many chances to take and make as we talk and paint that we can even give instances of what we cannot give instances of. The complete circle enclosing nothing.

Painting of a circle with the thinnest line. Two colours oppressing each other, advancing, warring, retreating and saying to each other NOTHING. And to paint it broken. Broken in tangents, ellipses, chords, hyperbolas, parabolas, never touching, all the functions of the circle never touching. Very clear and clean where they do not quite meet. The large four corners forcing the breakup into the painting. The attack of the square. But yes, there is a relationship all over the painting; the meld of each colour into itself in slow vague subtle rolls and blots and splotches and mottles. The battle of the colours within themselves not to be affected and yet being affected by the other. Many greens and one green, many reds in one red, but no orange goddamned red. Hateful colour, weaselly, ratting, turncoat colour. Yet every soft green and all the other reds. There is a title: Every soft Green and All the Reds but Orange. Beautiful to do. Very clear and careful. Thought out for once. Painting of André and me. Cool.

So there is a way. You can break it up all you like and they never do touch, but this one has its shape because of that one, and so the other too, and you seeing, join them.

Underpainting. Sizing canvas. What to paint where the colours do not meet. Jesus. Stop. And do it acrylic on glittering steel. Tremendous. Perfect. The steel is what you see between. Or no. Too obvious. On glass. Superb. But flakes and won't last. Or plain effective white. What MUST it be to achieve Bach.

Oh it will be something Harry. Don't go getting those bloody excuses again: I'm going to achieve this great one just as soon as I figure out one crucial detail. It doesn't matter. Just air between. Just the thin line of your renowned collection of kingwhiskers artfully laid on end to end.

How long have I been painting? Lost in the soup. There it is, not looking too bad on the easel. Walk round it now. What time is it? Hungry? Leave the bastard and go, but wait. Check the sketches. Yes. Now just turn on the overhead light and see it. Jesus. It looks awful. Quick, douse the light. Seen in half-light it is not too bad. What light did I have on when painting it? Is it any good? I can't tell.

Just into the can and unwind the bumwad around myself like so, easy to wind back on again round and round my waist as I have this spyglass. Now with the paper tube ready to gaze at it one-eyed. Turn the light on without looking at it and stand as far back as I can go with this round white middle and examine. Carefully approach watching each corner as I go. Amazing how this gives you objectivity. Yes. There I have definitely boobed. There. Sloppy and mediocre. What clichés I can do in paint when I don't watch out. But this is the start of my show, yes it is. I can feel the old build-up again, starting to work. I can take off in a hundred directions from this painting and never look back. Fascinating how the corners

"It is an appropriate costume."

"André. Hey, great, look at this."

"But why do you wipe yourself on the canvas with so much of that around?"

"Hey, it's not bad, eh? What do you think?" What does he think. Scarcely looks at it.

"I brought you new plates."

"Plates?"

"For the machine."

"Oh yes. What do you think?" And point again. "Original?"

"Hm." Watches. Walks around. Now to unwind this damned paper. Tear it off and rags to me stuck.

"It is articulate." Jesus. What does that mean?

"Do you like it?"

"I am surprised." He actually likes it. The old heron.

"Great. I'm working up a show from it. I think I'll call it Nuances. Or Nuages. Will you stay for dinner? I'm dying for company."

Interesting brown parcels he is carrying. Soothe him up and share some thoughts together over the dinner in the bags.

"I can't, Harry. I'm on my way. But keep care of this, will you? I must be off."

And goes, just like that. Damnit. The Frenchman ought to have made dinner. Steack au poivre. Bit of delicious salad. Crusty rolls. The lovely crackling brown bag he brought to my hunger and took away. Yes. Well now. I had a bag of peanuts here a while ago. Good old me willing to live on this. . . . But no. Not tonight. To celebrate Shirley's kindness. I know. Call Janine. Ask her to dinner. A kindness to us both. Do André a good turn trying to win her back. Oh, yes, sharing my bubble of joy round about the world. A kind fellow I am and full of unreasoning joy. Now, out with the lights. Close the window. Leave all shipshape. Locking the door carefully with the key he has given me. Should I spruce up for her? A pause thoughtful on the winding stairs. And no, because this is not a date but a kindness to us all. All four of us as it used to be those times in Paris. Out the wide black door at the bottom onto the cement yard stretching to the wasteland at the back covered with rubble. The evidence of our summed apathy. The lash of this damned little branch in the face at the door. Must fix that. Ho ho round the front and happily down the street towards the Bell Telephone building where all the pretty and single girls come hopefully out each afternoon looking for

Cops. Cars. Each end of street passing me. Cops going for

the studio. Cars stopping there with flashing lights revolving atop. Six cars. Must stop running. Stop. Running before I knew it. Slow down Harry. Stop here. Where will I go? André don't go there tonight. I should go back to see if they catch him. Stopping at this corner. Are they here waiting for me. Just walk boldly round the corner. Nobody. Back to the corner and look again. André, this is for real. Police.

Get away while I can. But where? My God, just walking out like that. Ten seconds sooner, and they'd have had me. Get going while I can along the street. Get towards Ste. Catherine. Where I can get into a crowd. So naked walking along here known suddenly to them searching for our press. The documents André left, the books and magazines and oh, did I leave anything signed there.

There's one now. Standing at the corner. Cross the street to avoid him. Now don't get me for jaywalking. Run Harry Run. A bullet in your back. Where will I go.

Janine. Run away from this back to you. You'll take me in. Yes. Into this crowd at the corner. Get lost in this friendly crowd. Buy a paper. Superb idea. Just like everyone else. Yes. Not *Devoir*. *Star*. Stay Anglo. Safe. Now walk along towards the lights. Scanning the headlines to see if I have been arrested yet. Not yet. Here. Bus stop. Onto this excellent bus. Get going towards the lights and more downtown confusion. Sirens. More cars coming with the lights. Man standing beside me as the bus suddenly stops to let the cops go by.

"It's these goddamned Separatists again, I bet. Throwing bombs." He has looked at my *Star*. His red loyal face. What to say to him? "Yeah, and the Pope's maiden name was Silverfarb, too." Off the bus and away walking. To find Janine and call André. If she knows.

In past the great cars to the door that retreats at your touch. Zooming in my painter's rags to the twentieth floor. It's probably a crime to wear such clothes in here. Crime of poverty.

"Harry. Come in." With a swoop and a gesture. Flying silk something or other. In.

"The police came to the studio."

"Oh my God, no."

"Exactly. I just got out with my blood still in me." Slightly rearranged since entering here. "I have to get in touch with him."

"Did they find him?"

"No. He's at some meeting. He said he wouldn't be back to-night."

"I knew this would happen someday. I knew it. Oh, he will be hurt. Everyone will be in it. They will find out everything."

"Where can we get him?"

"I don't know. The only place I know is the studio. No, wait a minute. The bookstore. You could go there."

"The bookstore?"

"Here, I'll show you." To the vasty sea-edge balcony tiny under our feet and not well enough railed at the edge of this drop. "Down that street, you see, and over two blocks, past the tall building."

"What's it called?"

"Le Marquis."

"Peculiar name."

"Maquis, with an R for revolution. Set behind the façade of propriety so the police won't guess. You can be over and back in a few minutes."

"I shall return."

"I'll be waiting," and her grey-green sea-green eyes both alive and steady on me. Flare of orange round her. Careful boy, you come back only with the message. But on wings of light I go down the corridor elevator street trying not to remember too hard, her. Not mine. But just to be nice and somewhere to stay. My indubitable charms that ought to be worked. Saving my love for yoo-hoo. Now around here and watch for it coming along. Pretty street this with the leaves hanging all about and the stone steps rising block after block in this faded purple light. Fine old bay windows as well and stone all about. City of stone where all is hidden. Yes. Five five five and up the steps. Tiny wooden sign across door Le Marquis. Yes. In and to the right without watching too closely for fear of what they will screw out of me afterwards in the dark confines. Bell. Loaded with books face out down the long rows.

"Yes sir?" His ascetic young face menacing. Blue turtleneck sweater of revolution. Black eyes in white face, bad teeth probably. Fu-rench all right.

"I'm looking for André."

"André?"

"Yes. André Riancourt."

"I'm sorry there is no one here named André Riancourt."

"I was told he would be here."

"I'm sorry."

Quick look about. Nobody. "Listen, the police have found his studio and his press. I must warn him."

"Well I think so. But perhaps you should tell the police when you find him, eh?"

"No, look. I am his friend. I have just come from the studio. He asked me to live there and watch out. Then Janine told me to come here."

"I'm very sorry sir. I cannot help you."

Standing looking at me quite unruffled.

"Would you care to look at a book, sir?"

"Please tell him will you."

"I can't help you sir. I don't know the gentleman."

"Well. Good day."

"Goodbye, sir."

Out. An excellent front if anything. Maybe I should wait in case he tells André inside. Hang about let André look out. Slowly across the street and back. Look up at the grey window. Five minutes. Should I leave for dinner? Or wait for André. Still nothing. I must press on. Re-enter. Same face. Same blank look. God, maybe it is not a front, and this guy will put them onto me. Fast out. His startled expression as I turn to go without a word. Stopping. Let 'em know we're not extinguished.

"I like your books. You've got a good name too. On se

maquille en marquis si l'on a l'air noble." Oh oh oh, that Air is inspired. Got him. He looks it. Watchful.

"What did you say?"

"You know." Have I hit a password maybe? I should have been an agent-double. Staring at him. Him looking mildly back. "I shall recommend you to André for the croix de guet." Mon Dieu, if that elision doesn't get him, nothing will. And still his quiet look changing to a smile for me poor fish.

"Very clever. I enjoy your humour sir."

"Oh well. Tell André will you?"

Down the steps slowly with my head down sense of failure. If they find him. Maybe this was not the place, after all. Find a dime in these shaggy greyjeans and phone Janine. And this fine aluminum box just nicely set up here under the leaves for calling terrorist messages privately through the searching city. How the innocent buses vroom by with their stink and whoosh and their undersea lights on. Montreal best at night with all its lights.

"Hello, Janine?"

"Yes. Harry, just a minute."

Christ, a siren. Kick open the door and ready to run. The more civilized bells of London. Flash flash down the street. Damn lights. Cop or ambulance. Cop going by. Still going by. More death downtown? I heard no bomb.

"Hello, Harry?"

"Yes, look, hang on. There's cops around here. Listen, I might have to run."

"Come back here."

"Yes, look, they don't know André here."

"What did they say?"

"Never heard of him. Are you sure . . . ?"

"Was it a short boy in black, with black hair and a thin face. Very sardonic look?"

"Yes."

"He'll tell André. They have to be careful now. Did you give him my name?"

"Yes."

"It will be all right."

"Should I stay here, in case he comes out?"

"No. It will be all right."

"It seems strange, inconclusive."

"It will be all right."

"Okay."

"'What will you do now?"

"I don't know."

"Have you a place to stay?"

"Not exactly."

"You could stay here." What to say to my disloyal feelings.

"Harry?"

"Yes. Thank you."

"Will you come?"

"I'd like to. It's very generous of you." Afraid to, now.

"Not at all."

"Goodbye, then, I'll see you shortly."

"Goodbye."

This secretive feeling putting up the phone. Not to be glimpsed now by André going out of here with glee on my shaking chops heading for a good dinner and a soft bed. In a wide flat in a tall building looking lazily over the lights relaxing with a beautiful girl beside me on the balcony. Private world suspended like a box seat over the beautiful city. To take a little of my own into it.

Swift detour into that liquor store I all too obviously remarked en route. Simply a kindly gift to the beautiful hostess. Nothing disingenuous at all. Offer it to André in case he decides to walk in. As I am walking swiftly now. Christ, I'm going fast. Must slow to a normal tread. Feet like springs bouncing. Damnit, Harry, you are not going to an assignation. Zorch. André sticking a bomb up my ass as I sleep. Generations of the finest going to glory. Oh no you don't, you stupid rev. For all my fine and pleasant lusts, I am not a bloody fool. This is simply her kindness to a desperate man whose whereabouts are becoming all too known. Let them be known tonight, but not too far. Just a small bottle of this good Armagnac for old times' sake, and have a shot André walking in the door, here's to your fine old streak of revolution, and here we were just sitting here talking about Vatican Three.

The Apartment

And with the Armagnac safe under my arm in brown
paper he advances carefully to his doom. Room.
She's too thin anyway, and what's a touch of this and that
to make a chap abandon his ancient fealties riding in an
elevator into this damned gantry. Pressed about with these
hard walls and eight-foot kneelings. Look down the hall and
the other end is you crouched under the weight of a thousand
bedrooms. Oh how quickly she answered the door and closed
it behind me and took the parcel and talked with that secon-
dary meaning of a woman about to be approached.

"Shall I make you some dinner?" And her standing just that
many feet away in her slippery orange blouse with the air of
knowing what distance separates us.

"Do you know what I would like more than anything?" To
approach you.

"No what?" Her amused smile.

"A bath."

"Certainly." Brisk, to the point, and for the first half second,
disappointed? God, get me out of here with my ikons still on
the shelf. She is bloody well determined to dust them off and
admire them as she strokes them. Bloody good thought to
masturbate in this brittle bathroom. Then I would be mechan-

ically safe from her at least for ten minutes. Undressing reluctant to lock the door for its degree of hope. Or insult.

Asleep in the deep. Perform my jaded miracle to old tunes. Stand up weak with hot water and lack of love to shower me off as the old water drains my scrofulous few days and hours and last minutes into the great long redgreen river below. By God I am fighting the good fight so far. Why then am I washing myself so carefully, as if expecting something all too dramatic later on. Think your vile thoughts you crowded jury of the past, you made all these mistakes too, and I have given a good ten minutes worth of myself so far.

"I'm in the kitchen. You can use my dressing gown if you like. Slippers in the cupboard."

H. Summers on the interpretation of schemes. Once for me into your clothes, dear lady, and the second time is easier, eh? With you in them this time. And why didn't you say André's slippers? Because they are not so long? Whose? My own clothes regardless, though I concede to the former's slippers.

"This is very pleasant, Janine." Seated at the table by the window with the door to the balcony open. "I haven't been so content for months."

"You are very welcome."

"This is delicious."

"Now, where are your things?" This hausfrau competence taking me over as she gets up from the table with a surprisingly hippy move and stands one hip down looking down at me. Her wide pale face and the body-consciousness of her as she stands.

"Yes. Well, at the studio."

"We could go down there and see if the police are still about. No, that might be too dangerous." Likes danger that girl. As she scoops up the plates and off the balcony with them talking into the living room speaking to me from there. Now moving back with the dessert. Watching me as I like it.

"Do you like it?"

"Yes, it's beautiful. What is it?"

"It's a Hungarian dessert. My mother is Hungarian. My father is Canadian – French."

"Really? Do they live here?"

"Yes."

"How did you get this apartment then?"

"It's my sister's. She is back in Budapest for a visit. The house is in Westmount. I decided to take this for – a while. Isn't it a glorious night?"

"Yes, very nice, Janine." And her leaning unnecessarily far over the table so I can see far into her orange fastness lighting her pale skin with the little white walls restraining her. How she arches her back as she straightens up and still stands with the hungry pose looking over me now pretending she is un-aware of me looking with her green eyes over the city. So near I can reach out and follow the curve of her hip under the skirt with one hand. Rising to get away from her. She not moving. Standing awkwardly on this cramped balcony unable to get by without touching her or saying excuse me. Which she does not want said. Waiting. She does not move, but carries on about this beautiful view. Yes it certainly is beautiful. Turns with her strong smile at me asking to share her joy in it. "It's so nice just to be able to stand here enjoying it isn't it? So peaceful." Tilt of her head to one side signifying she enjoys it.

"Let's do the dishes now so they are out of the way?" With what sweetness she asks. Out of whose way?

"Of course."

And into the glaring kitchen where her blouse is not quite thick enough to withstand the light. How haphazard and ex-cessive and sloppy she is doing them, splashing water. Clat-tering things. Turning all the time talking, smiling, enjoying. Looking down fondly affectionately at a dish which she washes like the face of someone she loves. Amazing. Turns every now and then carelessly close to me reaching around to do some-thing. Oh lady look, you're not my size. Do you know that?

Hang up the towel and wander in indecisively to the dark-ened living room. About to turn on the light as she sweeps the curtain open. "Let's not turn on any lights. I like to watch the city."

"Okay, Janine." At last, apart, on separate chairs. She does not seat herself warmly close, at least.

Let a few minutes of guestly propriety slip by. "Well, I guess I should go along."

"Where?" Now a dreamy tone.

"Well, to a boarding-house I know."

"But you're going to stay here."

"I am?"

"Of course. What kind of a boarding-house?"

"Well, I stayed there a little while when I first came. A fraternity house."

"But you were living in the studio."

"Yes."

"But you haven't kept the other room?"

"No."

"Well, then stay here. It will be uncomfortable at the boarding-house, won't it? And cost you money? And food?"

"Yes."

"Well, why shouldn't you stay here? As long as you need?" Getting up and doing things to the sofa. "You can sleep here. You must be tired. It's big enough for you and no one will know you are here."

"Meaning the police."

Laughing. "Look." Holding up stripey somethings. "I have an old pair of pyjamas you can have. They're too big for me. My brother's." Harry, really, she is being damned nice to you. Up and say something nice to her, you suspicious bastard. "Janine, you are being very kind. Thank you. I am very grateful."

"Nonsense. It's only sensible. Besides, I enjoy it. Now, here's a pillow. Do you like two? Close the curtains if you like. A light here if you want to read. You can use my sister's toothbrush, by the basin. We can have breakfast on the balcony. It looks like a nice night. I'll be in the bedroom if you need anything." And her wandering away casually. Singing as she presumably changes. Brushes. Flushes. Begins to cease her clatter. Presumably settles. As I lie here in the dark sensing the crack of light below her door, and gradually drift off unharmed. To pass a day here hiding alone and away resting from the world with this bright bird singing about. Her black hair and her enthusiasm. Perhaps her motions around here are all unconscious. She made no overt move. Yet I have the feeling she would either accept my advance quite commonsensibly and do the right thing, or she would be astounded. She is just taking care of me like a good-hearted mammy. No more in it than that. Into this delicious state of dreams unbidden hazily floating into my head possessing me. Beautiful colour. Peace.

Quietly walking past me. Casually. Nightgown. Out the door and breeze over my bare feet. Cover them. Smoking a cigarette out there alone. To lie here unbidden. Waiting. Staying a marvelously long time out there. Whisper "Janine?" Nothing. Louder: "Janine?" Out beside her. No surprise. But a smile for me. "Smell the flowers. You can smell them at night." Little white blossoms unfolded. In their box.

"They're nice. What are they?"

"Nicotine. They only smell at night."

"Yes." Turning and looking up at me. My hands. Stop. Not actually touching her. Turning away. But her hands coming to cover mine on the cool railing. Oh my God. Stand stiffening unable to turn to her. Just a friendly gesture. Looking dark-eyed up at me. "Janine. Oh, Janine." And touching her waist through this thin nothing. This friendly girl is all under there. Willingly turns to me and allows me to kiss her head lifted to me. Lifting so I can kiss her forehead. Still friendly. But insisting on her lips. Lifting her face to me and stepping closer to me. Pressing herself against me. Kissing me rising. On her toes to me. Pressing and pressing. Kissing her lips open to me. Kissing a flower. Arms around me holding me. Wanting me. Trying to get away from this awkward kiss and beautiful closeness. "Janine, oh Janine, you are so great." Her arms under my arms reaching up to pull me down and kiss her again. Again breaking free of her flower grasp to talk into her alien hair very black. "You are so alive. Beautiful." She seems to want only to kiss. How close she holds and presses full of love. Love? Rubbing herself on me gently. Like a cat. Gently moving against me. My God. Only her pale nightie. "Oh Janine." Bending down to right-arm behind her two knees and swirl her up. Arms around my neck and kissing my neck as we go. Knock her feet against the door. Uncaring of her. Into the living room. To the sofa.

"Not here. The bedroom." Kissing my ear. Little nibbles. To the bedroom with no light on but this from the city below casting light shadows. Settling her on the bed and her arms still round my neck pulling me down and coiling round on the bed for me beside.

"Janine." No.

"Mmm. Harry." Little hums for her and swishing her legs cat's tail over the sheets. Too hot, too sensuous. She only wants. Not enough. Right. But down beside her and her stretching out hard to her toes reaching toward me and pulling me on. Pale face smiling from the dark hair. Beauty of the night. My God, I am about to. Her hands. What is she doing. Stretching as she pulls up her nightie and bares herself putting it over my face kissing me through it. Turns on top of me bare kissing me through this lace mess. God what resources she has. Covering my face with kisses as she pulls it off.

"Janine."

"What is it my darling? My darling." Kisses my cheeks and cruises round to my ear not quite letting me see her nakedness but lifting so I glimpse down a bit.

"What is it love?"

"Fine. Superb. Nothing." My hands down her silk back. Smooth. The rise to her bottom I can't quite reach.

Her rising on her hands looking down at me and her bosom tiptouching me, hair falling about her face in the beautiful frame of love. As she drops to kiss me her bosom drops with her pressing down. No. I can't. Not now.

Oh, the pleasure she has given me. The gratitude. But away to the bathroom. Shame. No lights. Quick as I can and back to her lying on the bed turning with a smile. I can hear her lips part with a tiny pop with this wonderful smile bringing me back to her arms crooning and pressing my head to her just below her chin and stroking my head. What an amazing girl. Both all pleasured except for these dangerous dearests of hers. Now if she will just not demand something more, this will have been only in the nature of medicine. But I owe her this move, and she takes it and accepts it. Oh the distress of giving pleasure in this way. The harsh mechanical nature of it. Avoiding sin as you commit it. If she would not emit these cat-calls. Her nature to do it lying pleasuring herself on the bed against all advice. But yet a stirring pleasure to do it for her. Kisses repeated after passion. Trying to act the tender part with her. Kissing her face afterwards. I'll not stay the night in your bed.

"Goodnight, sweetness."

"Where are you going?"

"To the sofa."

"No. Come here."

"Well, just a minute." Into the washroom again. A hard night for the plumbing. Goodbye little sofa, I really tried. Back to her. Still not in her verdammt nightie. Under one sheet, me and her. And the small rain doth rain. Shirley, André, never find me out. I can play it all right from here, getting away whole, knowing what I know now. This curled body beside me warming up beside me. Extend comfort to her in the agony of her loneliness, in the need of her hausfrau nature. Only an extension of her housely kindness. To get away and wipe the sin from my face. But it will never wash off. Anyway, it was a pleasure. Really a pleasure. How warm her lips and body were. Well, all over, and back to work. To the real world where things like this do not happen to a faithful loving Harry. I do love you Harry and André and Janine and Shirley. Who could believe it? I do.

"Janine."

"Yes sweet."

"This has been darling." And never again.

"Mm hm." And within the hour we do it superbly again.

Believe me my loves, I love you all the more. Releasing myself. Just lovely lying here with you, and all the world in you. Love.

How to circle round her whichever morning this is and be cheerful knowing it is no good between us. It must be Shirl and I must phone her quickly or die of fear. Of longing. Even these few nights with Janine have proved sordid because we are only lonely with each other and giving skin comfort without sustenance. My talk with her this morning is wooden and banal, and we are not in love. Yet I am grateful to her looking over the coffee at her pointed and quick face on the balcony in this lovely April weather.

"What month is this, Janine?"

"July."

"It feels like April this morning. It is your presence upsets the seasons."

Smile from her. Yet not sentimental, not clinging to me. Just acknowledging. Any moment now I expect to hear you say "Harry you are a sweet boy." But it is only Shirl and what do I say to this other? Does she expect me to stay here and nirp all day? Rather pleasant at that.

"Will you be all right here? I am going down there for a while to the Musée."

"I have to run along to the studio." And when shall we meet again.

"The studio?"

"Yes. I'm in the middle of something. I'm working. . . ."

"The police."

"Oh. Will they still be there? I guess so, eh?"

Wonderful soft laughter turning hoarse at me. I guess I've boobed again.

"You'd better stay away completely, don't you think?"

"Damn. Yes. Don't you think I . . . no. Will they still be there? Why would they hang around?"

"To see if anyone comes round. I must go now. I'll be through about nine o'clock tonight." The significance of that. Janine, you are becoming like my sister and I do not want to fuck you all this time. "Have a good day, and please let me clean up," as she starts to clear away. "You just go on and I'll be the dishwasher."

"Thank you." Simply said. And off she goes in street clothes as if I belonged here after these few days. We are not clinging to each other. But I'm trapped. My whereabouts are becoming known. This kind of girl a man could love. Funny how we skip the morning kiss which belongs to another couple. Not us. And for a moment to stand on the great balcony looking over the city ready to call Shirley. Avoiding dishes here. But call, Harry, call while you have the chance.

I have left it too long this day. Delayed. Janine will be home soon. Nine soon. Call, Harry, call against this daylong fear and sloth. Call. To the phone and finally fearfully calling.

Where will she be sitting when I call? Surprise. My perfervid imaginings. In a ballgown her gentle eyes misting with tears as she sits on the edge of something listening to my love words. I must not and I must all walking back and forth. Agony making sweat. No more thought. Yes operator, overseas. Yes, I do not know the number. Yes in London. Yes, Maddiver on Pont Street. Yes, of course it is late in London. It is late everywhere. Yes it is an emergency. Yes go on. I need strength to cross the Atlantic with these incredible words. The answered ring. I know her mother's voice. Canada. Of course. Coming. God she is coming to the phone. Hearing as plain as

"Shirley?"

"Hello?"

"Shirley, it's Harry. Can you hear me?"

"Perfectly."

"I had to call. I am overwhelmed. I apologize for the lateness. Will you talk?"

"Of course. What's the matter?"

"I'm not sick. I'm not going to apologize just yet. I mean, are you alone?"

"Yes, I'm on the phone in the library."

"Shirley, look. I've been waiting." Wait. Nothing. "Shirley?"

"I'm still here."

Buzzing of the presumed waves.

"Did you get my letter?"

"Yes, thank you."

"You sound so composed. I'm breaking up."

"I'm not composed. I can hardly speak."

Thank you Shirley.

"I love you. Can you come over here?"

"Oh Harry." Do I hear her voice so light through this? What to read in it?

"Shirley, I'll send you all the rest of the money. Can you come?"

"I don't know."

"Do you want to?"

"Yes." And low.

"Did you say yes?"

"Yes. Yes."

"Then come."

"I don't know. Yes, oh Harry, I'll try."

"Thank you. Please come as soon as you can."

"Harry, do you mean this? It's not just another of your momentary things?"

"Yes Shirley, it is. That's exactly what it is. But it's okay. Really. I can explain it to you here much better. Alter caelum. . . ."

"What?"

"It means I'm your man in Latin. In Canada. But I need you alone. Can you understand that?"

Her superb laughter. Able to laugh just now.

"You mean at your mercy."

"Exactly. As now telephoning, I am at yours. You will come?"

"Yes."

"Now you must take my address." And giving her André's address. This phone number conveniently written here. And the fraternity address just in case. She already has mother's address in Port Faith.

"We must hang up Harry. This is costing you a fortune."

"I love you and love you and love you. Please come as fast as you can. Do you want me to get the ticket here?"

"I'll let you know. We must hang up if you're going to pay for it."

"Don't give a damn. I'm totally euphoric just to hear you again. But I do believe what you say. Now I promise to hang up quickly. Cable fastest, and I'll meet you. For God's sake fly. Now I'll promise to hang up. I love you and goodbye. Fly, Shirley."

"Goodbye."

No click.

"Shirley?"

"Yes."

"I can't let go. Any minute, I'll kiss this phone."

"Oh Harry. . . ." Sound of her stifling. Laughter? Weeping?

"Please, please. I wait every instant that I cannot hear you."

"Goodbye Harry." Scarcely able to speak. At last savagely pressing down the button. Quick up. "Shirley?"

"Are you finished sir?" Gone. Gone. Gone. Flomp it down. Onto the floor. My first prayer in ages. Thanks be to God who has done all this. And lying on my back singing Holy Holy Holy, Lord God Almighty. The marvels of love across the ocean. But how I lusted even as I loved. How earlier I loved even as I lusted. Damned weird nature we have. Singing Holy Holy Holy and not the sign of obscenity in it but gratitude.

The feet down the corridors pass this door and they are not Janine's. I might as well be the unfaithful husband awaiting the death knell for all the loyalty I have twice displayed today. Must rid myself of this contorted mess I am in before it strangles me. Dead Harry with a thousand things yet undone in life. What to say to Janine as she comes in the door. Finally is here opening it slowly and looking for me. In the darkness awaiting her.

"Hi."

"Hello Harry. Are you all right?"

"In a manner of speaking."

Janine putting down bags carefully quietly as if she knows and does not want to upset me more. "Harry, I spoke to André."

"You did? Where?"

"He has not been to the studio. He is okay. He got our message."

"Oh. Thank you."

"He wants to see you at the bookstore tonight."

"About the radio station?"

"Yes. I told him I would give you the message."

"Does he know?"

Her shrug. Does Janine care? Is this becoming permanent between us? "Janine." Coming up to Janine, coming up to her with hands to her waist, thin waist to lightly hold her without possessing. Careful Harry. This is all changing very fast and you do not understand it yet.

"Janine, what did you think when you talked to him?"

Looking away, not able to tell me. It is too hard for her. "Don't tell me if you don't want to." Her eyes seeming to see too far just now, almost with tears. "He is my husband." To take my hands away from another man's wife. Stand ashamed. "No Harry, I did not mean it that way. Come here." Giving me with her eyes open this sweet thoughtful kiss.

"You seem to think when you do that, Janine?"

"Do I?" And slowly giving me another. Fills me with wonder. What is this kiss of yours, Janine, what does it mean now?

"I didn't tell him you were here. I didn't want him to know."

"Must I see him?"

"I don't want you to. Because you are indiscreet."

"I swear I don't want to tell him. Now. But I will be nervous. How can I lie. What can I say?"

"Tell him you were at the boarding house. Let him think I telephoned you. But don't tell him. Not now."

And to confess that Shirley is coming. That we can be free of this and harmless. But as she stands so close and seems to need me. . . . "Janine. . . ." Like a knife in her. How to begin. . . .

"I am going, Janine."

"Yes, you must. He will be waiting there soon."

"Janine, I mean I called Shirley today. She is coming."

"Here? When?"

"I'm not sure. Soon."

"How do you know?"

"I called her." Going round the flat putting things away. Flopping down not quite tired. Smiling at me.

"I don't wonder."

"What do you mean?"

"You are an attractive man, Harry."

"She is too. So are you. I feel great. Shall we dine out? I've got loot."

"Did you tell her where to come?"

"I think so. Oh, the studio. But I gave her this number, I think."

"Harry, Harry. Did you phone from here?"

"Yes." Long-distance charges.

"Then you read the number off the telephone?"

"Yes."

"Cable her right away."

"Yes. Of course. Why?"

"If she goes to the studio, Harry, oh dear. You are so hopeless. Really." And lying back in total laughter on the sofa looking absolutely superb. But not tonight, Harry, not tonight. "Here is your abandoned bride faithfully coming to a police trap." Laughter again too long. She does not feel it. Sounds wild, hysterical. Watch it Harry, now she looks mad. Lies there casually looking out the window. What to do or say? Harry has done it again, boobed on an impulse. To stand here waiting for the inevitable punishment. And what a way to have told her. Right in the face like a snowball when she comes in. How to make it up? Gently ask her "Would you like a drink?"

No answer. Brooding she is. Fixing up a real devastator to blow me out of the water. Here it comes. A sigh and aims it out the window.

"Harry, you are so amazing." Play it cosy.

"I am?"

"Why did you come here if you intended to call her?"

"I didn't know I was going to call her."

"But you must have."

"Honestly, no." What can I say? "I wrote to her."

"When?"

"I don't know. A couple of days ago, I guess. Couple of weeks. I don't know."

"Are you so ignorant?"

"I beg your pardon?"

"Don't you know what goes on in your own mind?"

"No. Not always."

This silence as she gets up and we walk round each other almost literally. Passing up and down the living room floor. Is she going to fight and throw me out?

"Janine, I honestly didn't know. I didn't intend to embarrass you." And you did want me to be kind to you and come into your bed and it was wonderful for you and me. It was great. "I guess being here with you made me see what I wanted." That sounds awful. She looks very coolly at me now. "If you imagine I did not want you Janine, allow me to lead you in there." To the great bed.

"But not every night. You wouldn't want me past a weekend?"

"How could it be?"

"Do you mean André?"

"Yes, partly."

"I don't know then. I don't know what would have happened, Harry. But I didn't expect this. No. I did not expect you to do this."

"Janine, the truth is . . ." What? Not sure.

"I am convenient, eh?"

"God, no. You woke me up. I was dead when I came here. I had no hope. You made me feel wonderful again."

"A little bit too wonderful."

"You mustn't be like that."

"Well what is it then? It was all over between you and Shirley, you said."

"I did? I don't remember saying that. Perhaps. I thought it was, for a while. Honestly, until I came here. Then, you were so nice, and helped me. . . ."

"A bit too much."

"Janine, please, I am not being cynical."

"I'm sorry. I come home like this, and you tell me so excited Shirley is coming. What am I supposed to do? Look happy and prepare for a ménage à trois. Harry, you are a very naïve boy."

"I see. I'm sorry."

"Do you think life is a toy, that you pick it up and set it down whenever you want?"

"I don't know."

"Well it isn't. You live all the time whether you like it or not. That's why I wanted you here. You had to have somebody. I had to have somebody. You don't put life down whenever you like. It has too many people in it."

"I didn't mean to."

"Well, that is exactly what you are doing."

"I know. I mean, I didn't mean to use you."

"Yes? Good for you. But you are just picking up this part of your life and playing round with it, and I'm in it Harry, I'm part of it and it's no good. Oh, you're crazy. There's no point in this."

Don't give up Janine, I mean to learn.

"Yes, I know. Can't do anything usual, and it doesn't bother me. That's the only part that bothers me." Why do I say such things. I don't want to be flippant.

Standing around, occasionally looking at me. I think she may believe that last bit. God knows it's sort of true.

"Crazy like a baby. You just haven't grown up. I wish I could teach you something."

"It would be nice. I was a virgin until last night."

"You've been here over a week." And suddenly laughing. "What did you learn? But I don't believe you."

"I was. Really." This is too embarrassing. Make her sound like a whore. What a time to be shy about it. "I guess I found out you were loving."

"Loving." Looking cynical.

"Janine, you look so suspicious. Please. I can't tell you when you look like that." How defensive she suddenly is. "I just meant you were sympathetic. Open to me. Friendly. You knew without being told. You didn't make me rehearse all my pain. Do you see what I mean? I didn't have to prove it to you." Oh, she must believe.

"I'm sorry, Harry. I see. Don't be upset."

Tears in my eyes trying to convince her I value you. "I do Janine, I prize you, I never want to hurt you, you don't know what you have meant to me, peace, happiness, honour, hope again. You have been just wonderful, and I adore you and I do love you, and I would defend you against anything." Sounds melodramatic. But her green eyes are full looking at me. She believes. "You see that's what I mean, I didn't have to prove it to you, you just accepted me. You brought me back to life. I believe in it again." Okay, don't overdo it Harry. You weren't exactly a basket case. Smile at her at this thought, and she reads it the right way. Get up and kiss her hand, you clumsy fart. Doing it as gracefully as twenty years in Port Faith allow. I have reached her and she believes. This is better than bed. At least you don't have to clean up afterwards. What an oaf I am. She smiles and shrugs and I bet she could share these comic thoughts if I tried. But you have boobed enough tonight

Harry, and don't mock the poor girl till she gets over finding out that you are three times nuttier than she imagined.

"You see, Janine, I have lived all my emotional life in Sud Ontario, and I'm only just now recovering. It's sort of like being encased in plaster for a hundred years. When you finally get out it takes a few seconds to limber up."

"Thank you, Harry. You see I am not casual in my emotions."

"No." Looking seriously at her, and she laughs at me. Making me feel gauche, but not exposed to you. Never again worried about you. "I feel happy. Is that okay, Janine?"

"That's fine." And smiling all right.

We have sexed too much. It is not really my part, but this friendly understanding is.

"I need a drink. Would you get me one?"

"Certainly." And able to say walking away "If you will believe it, I love you." Regardless of bed, and because of it. To hand this to her with a bow and a smile and a kiss neither chase nor lusting. "To you, Janine."

The Meeting

Once again up the grey steps, this time to be ushered
unexpectedly by long-hair in jeans up the inner
sanctum stairs. Atop which someone waits standing
looking down.

"André. Good to see you."

"Come in here. You're the first. The others will be along in
a few minutes."

And Harry, keep your big mouth shut this time about
Janine. Though of course, he knows I have seen her. But he is
saying nothing. Or is that why he brought me in here first.
Long narrow room with a lot of chairs against the walls. But
part sitting-room and that long couch down there is someone's
bed.

"Harry, I called you in first alone, because I want you to
understand the precise nature of what we are doing. The kind
of message we are going to broadcast is not new, but the
method is. Complete surprise. Nobody ever tried anything like
this before. It will be a demonstration of several things which
are psychologically important." How he is sitting with total
concentration and intentness watching me sharp as a bird. "Up
to now the movement has been sporadic, ill-defined, insub-
stantial. Now there will be a whole series of co-ordinated,

expert, well-planned blows at the establishment. Naturally I can't reveal the whole plan. Our part of it is very small. Necessarily, it is split into a number of small units, so that if any one part fails, the whole is not threatened."

"Right. But what are all these blows?"

"The only part that need concern us is the station. There will be a number of other things."

"But what is their nature?"

"The only ones I know of are purely demonstrations. But of a kind that has never been seen before in Quebec. In one night, there are planned sixteen various forms and kinds of demonstration. One group will attend a night sitting of the House of Commons in Ottawa, another the session of the Quebec Legislature. Special editions of the Separatist magazine have been printed, fifty thousand copies of one edition alone, and they will be distributed to selected people across the province, mayors, deputies, the main part of the political and social élite. There will be a demonstration at a federal Liberal party fund-raising rally here in Montreal. This is unique – nothing like this has ever been staged here before. But the most cunning thing is that there will be no way for the federalists to understand at first who or what is behind it. Some of the demonstrations are being planned by the MSA to secure support for their candidates in the election in September. The rest will appear to be something else – outbursts of public protest against Confederation on every level of society. The effect will be to drive even the most extreme Separatists into the MSA camp for at least one election, and at the same time, to prove to the middle-of-the-road voters that the old federalist parties have nothing to offer them, because all of the Separatists, of every kind, protest so vigorously against them. I tell you this is going to make le samedi de la matraque look like Bingo night at Our Lady of Perpetuity in Saint Tit. It will be an avalanche of protest. You see the effect?"

"How is it different from what has gone before? There have been demonstrations here before."

"But not on this scale, Harry, nothing planned and co-ordinated this way."

"How will that help?"

"Wait a moment. I haven't finished. The heart of the matter is just here. It is mass, you see, the effect will be to convince the authorities that this is it, the mass uprising they have feared all along. They are poised for this, they have battle plans, and the Quebec government has bought riot trucks and trained squads in riot dispersal, and the Canadian Army is ready to fly in troops if necessary. The idea is to provoke a massive response on all levels, scare the authorities into moving with all their forces. Then, our people are gone. They disperse, disappear. One hour after the whole thing starts, it is over. Our part is over. But by then, all the troops and riot squads are in motion, it is too late to stop them. Now, here is the key. They will find none of our people—the streets, the radio stations, all the key places, are empty of our men. Now the students come into it. There are hundreds of thousands of students in this province, plus the cadres of the labour movement. All sympathetic to us, in one way or another. If they move out, the police have only the innocent to arrest."

"Why innocent?"

"They are not part of it. They are deliberately excluded. All they have heard so far is rumour, there is a big thing planned for the night of August twelfth. Less than a month from now."

"But if they aren't told exactly what to do, they'll just mill around."

"Precisely. That is exactly what we want them to do. If the police are the slightest bit worried or upset, and the very scale and daring of this is bound to worry them, then when they see anyone looking suspicious, they will move. And all they will have caught in their net is people who know nothing. The thing is to play on their fears, heighten their anticipation, keep them off balance, and wait for them to make a mistake. That is why it is supremely important for us not to make the first mistake ourselves. And if they make the least error, we have six lawyers here in Montreal alone to fight cases of false arrest, to bring charges of police brutality, to capitalize on those charges that have already been laid in Quebec. With every newspaper headline, with every case of false arrest or whatever, they will look more and more like fools. It will be proven in the streets that they are unfit to govern. Do you know, in the entre'acte of *Le Bourgeois Gentilhomme* . . . what is that?"

Langevin coming in whistling. Jaunty as a bird.

"Langevin for Christ's sake cut the whistling. This isn't a goddamn play rehearsal."

"Hello, André, Harry." Langevin sauntering down the long room to us. "What's the matter with you tonight?"

"Listen Langevin, this is more serious than you seem to think."

"I'm here, aren't I, and on time?"

"That's not the point. This is one hell of a serious business, and you don't seem to realize it."

"I realize it all right." Sitting back casually on the sofa and gazing around.

"Look, you were supposed to meet me last night at Robert's, and where were you?"

"I sent a message. I had to go to a family party."

"Exactly. What the hell were you doing at a party when you should have been at the meeting?"

"André, you told us it was essential to keep up appearances, not to let the family know what was going on. I've already been out of the house every night for weeks, and this time my mother insisted that I stay. What could I do? I was only trying to keep her from becoming suspicious. I come home every night late, with my fingers stained with printer's ink, I can't get it off, and she wonders what the hell I am doing. I tell her I am out with Andréanne, and I forget to warn Andréanne, and she phones my mother to find out where I am, and it gets all very complicated. So. I sent you a message."

"All right, all right. I thought you just didn't give a damn. What have you told Andréanne?"

"Nothing much."

"What do you mean nothing much?"

"I asked her to trust me, and I said I was not going out with anyone else, and I had a big business deal going on which I couldn't tell her about, and you know, that sort of thing. What is this, anyway? You're treating me like a Mountie."

"We must be careful, we mustn't let anything go wrong. The lawyer told me it could easily mean fourteen years for conspiracy to defraud. If they try to charge us with sedition, the maximum penalty is life imprisonment."

"Fourteen years. Life. My God, they wouldn't try that."

"Goddamnit Langevin, I've told you and told you. Do you never learn?"

Poor old André sitting there while the shocked Langevin regards him. The embarrassment of his outburst. André leaning forward hands down to his ankles sitting on the old red couch trying to get over something.

"André," Langevin sounding concerned.

"I'm sorry. Never mind. It's just that this is perhaps the most serious thing that has ever happened to any of us, and it seems to be impossible to get that across, sometimes."

"I understand."

"All right then, listen." And André starts to outline our part, though his eyes suddenly seem small and tired. And he takes us through the dry run here, the little map and all. Until it's dark enough we wait now with Jean-Jacques and Philippe, smoking and drinking no more than one beer to go down to his car and drive out the streets with people all about paying no attention as we draw up in front of this old meeting hall. Out east somewhere. And André casually driving stops the car and pulls out his notes to me in the front seat and the others astern.

"Harry, you will pick us up here at ten fifteen. I am to attend a demonstration here against the Liberal party rally that will be held that night. The Prime Minister will attend and a couple of cabinet ministers, and probably some members of the Quebec Opposition. Harry, you park the car here at ten o'clock, and wait."

"What about the car?"

"I'm coming to that. It has not yet been arranged, but when

it is, I will let you know. Jean-Jacques, you and Langevin and Philippe arrive here separately by any means you choose except taxi. Under no circumstances take a taxi that night because you have no idea who will be driving. And watching. Harry, you wait here until I come out. You others, get in the car as you arrive, and keep your guitar cases with you. Don't put them in the trunk. I want us to be able to move to the station as fast as possible once we are parked. Now Harry, you take the wheel from here and drive us out."

Langevin leaning forward. "Should the car be any special kind to fit in with a promoter?"

"Probably yes. Go left up here Harry. And remember this route. We have to get there quickly." Winding north out of the city along Pie Neuf and the thousands of Louisiana iron balconies and thousands of paint shades and all the ghastly mediocrity of piled-up apartment living. Now hilled trees in the darkness and a winding drive up to the spread-out towers of station COFR.

"Along there Harry," André pointing along the pavement to the small building next the first tower. The aluminum letters above the door. "Now you park as close to the door as you can get, and we go in there. Back the car in so you can drive out straight ahead. That's right." Nobody about just now, but the lights on and a couple of cars parked over there.

"When you get out, open the trunk and reach in and get something out, anything, just pretend, and then leave the lid up, so it looks as if we will be back in a few minutes, and also to show that there is nothing difficult in there. Also leave the lid up when we go. Don't shut it."

"Why not?"

"If anything goes wrong, and they're running after us as we come out, they'll look at the back of the car as we go, and all they'll remember is the lid up, and they may not think to get the plates so quickly." A glance in the mirror from Langevin to me. This is ridiculous. The lid up? Surely we should do better than that. And that's exactly what Langevin is thinking. But he's afraid to go after André now. Do it, Harry.

A glance at André to test the air, but he is staring mournfully out the far window.

"André, we should have false plates, surely."

"Don't be melodramatic."

"Melodramatic. What do you mean?"

"Nobody knows what we are doing now."

"André, I meant on the night of the raid."

"Oh." Not looking at me. "Yes, it is possible."

"Maybe essential."

"Yes. Philippe, will you look after that please?"

"Okay." And we drive in silence back to the store. Remember this route, Harry.

And as we go back and park at the bookstore, the rapid instructions. Langevin taking over. Thank God he is showing his stuff now. And André silent. Getting the guitars on loan, the tape equipment, and me to phone this number Langevin hands me with my supposed name and the group name etched. Two of the members are in the U.S.A. playing dates, and they're just coming through town this night, and we are to use the taping equipment there to record broadcast quality for the audition. Must be this certain RPM and they haven't a studio of their own because they've been split up, but Langevin has played with a group that was on Ed Sullivan last month, and here is their name, and Langevin is actually Pierre Beausoleil whose name is in this issue of *Variety* he is handing me. "God this is thorough."

"Now your part is one we can't fake, Harry, so you'll just have to help as much as you can. This disc jockey has never heard of you, so you have to let on you're from Toronto or somewhere and just moving into Montreal to handle this group here, and a few others. You round up some names of groups in Toronto who haven't got a manager, real groups, mind you, if at all possible. This has to appear legitimate."

"Okay, I know a guy I can call who can give me some names."

At last it appears tout reglé and still André is sitting there, hardly having contributed. A firm goodbye to Langevin, who looks at André for me. I feel he believes in me at last. "Goodnight, Langevin, I'll see you next week." "Goodnight." And the glance telling me to stay with André. Close the door quietly on them and back to André slumped with his beer.

"André, what happened?"

"What do you mean?" But refusing to look at me.

"You hardly said a thing after that big build-up."

"I saw the station, and I knew we were going to fail."

"What are you talking about. That's the only way we will fail, if you refuse to believe success."

"I saw that place, and I thought how amateurish this all is, and at first I said to myself 'Let's see how Langevin and Harry make out' but I was fooling myself. What I felt was failure."

What a time to think that. What to say. Sitting mournfully not drinking his bottle, but idly swishing it back and forth with a peculiar little smile gazing up this long room to the far window full of neon in the distance. Is he pulling out? No time to pussy around with him.

"Are you pulling out?"

"No. No, I'll stay."

"How can we want you if you aren't convinced?"

"I am convinced."

"That we're going to blow the whole thing."

"No."

"Well, what then? What is it André?"

"Oh, I just saw this for what it is, a lot of bien pensants, or people who think they are, going against the current, amateurs with no understanding, ready to give up everything for a cause which is already lost. You see, if this were a real revolution, we wouldn't be playing around with tape recorders and signs and slogans, but with a true army to fight. And what chance would that have? This little thing will just be banter to the English, and to the capitalist French themselves. What we are doing Harry, is next best, it is not a choice we have, but a fate we despise. So after I talked to you, all the brave words,

I felt downcast, and then up against that solid building with the feebleness of our little effort, no matter how magnified, I felt despair. So I thought, I leave it to you two for tonight, you seemed fired up and ready to go."

"Oh, you meant, just for tonight."

"Yes." At last a look around at me. "You didn't think I meant to abandon you entirely at this stage."

"I thought that's what you meant. Yes."

"No, not tonight. Just for tonight, I allow myself the luxury of realism. Fatal when you are desperate. And, I thought about you, I wondered about you. I wanted to see what you would do tonight."

"Why?"

"Curiosity. A desire to see you in limbo, you see, up against nothing, forced to act."

"I've told you what I feel."

"Not entirely. I would admire you as a man of principle in all this, acting for something you believe in, in the most abstract sense, with nothing to gain but a reinforcement of your belief, I guess, I don't really know. That's the curious thing, I don't know."

"It is not principle, at least, I don't think it is. I don't know, or yes, sometimes I do. I used to think it was hate for the wrongly established order, but more, it is this, to see what is going on here and, not to react, not to want to act, and take part, is impossible. The old world is ending, and something new is happening, and this is for me. Someday maybe I'll be old, and I will hear myself asking, what did you do with your youth, what did you do when you were young and had the chance, did you make a difference, did you live through something really big and stay small yourself, did you just lie down and let history run over you, or by God when you had the chance, did you stand up and say, no, not this, and yes this. Adventure, all right, crazy, all right, but those get hurled at you whether or not . . . but I want to be known for what I did, and for knowing something when it happened, and seeing, at the time, and moving, at the time. And this is now for me.

Now for the whole country, and I'm tired of trying to think why, just look at it, you know what is happening. There is the reason why."

One clap of his hands. To signify the end. Finality.

"Remember. I didn't ask you for that."

"All right, that's what I feel, that's why I'm here. Now give me a beer, I'm dry. And get that mournful look off your face, boy, we're going in for a goal."

Yet I am forced not to be able to cheer him up, in my position with Janine. I cannot speak about her to him, and there is still the gap between us, once his Frenchness, and my Ontario strand, and now Janine. We can never cross it, but only change its name.

A weird night such as the three sisters would invent. The clouds race and it is hot and still below here. Pray for a cool wind out of the north. Blow all this smog away and let us breathe. Strange hot night full of fitful gusts and long silences while the city sounds burred around, aglitter in the air but unclear, like the soft furred surface of aluminum. To paint acrylic on aluminum.

And strange to have been driving a car again. How generous Janine is. I am caught by a finger, can't get away from her. Can't move properly for her hold on me. How generous she is, the apartment, the car, offers of money when I need it. Yet she manages to remain remote withal. Carefully to drive in without damaging this small car with the English shift, carefully into the mooring place at this very fine apartment, tie up and die the engine. Yes. With the key upstairs. It must be late. Lights out everywhere.

"How was it?"

"Thank God, I thought you might put me out."

"What's the matter?"

"I'm just relieved, that's all. I thought you were so mad, you would put me out tonight." And for her answer coming forward silently and slowly putting her arms round me and hands up my back and drawing me to kiss her. Large and even kiss. Well meant.

"You are a creature of surprises. Sometimes still, sometimes so quick. As now."

"Are you hungry?"

"Yes." Leading the way to the kitchen.

"What did you do?"

"We went to a planning meeting, and then to the radio station. It's a very complicated business." Giving me coffee. "Thanks." And croissants with honey. Superb. In the glare light of the kitchen quietly plotting more protest, outlining it all to her nodding head. She seems to fit into this, even approve.

"I thought you were against this, Janine?"

"There is something I didn't tell you. Now it is almost too late. I am ashamed."

"Why?"

"I am going back to André. I am going to help him all I can."

"I'm glad. Very glad, Janine." To reach across a kitchen table and hold her hand and look at her with this warm feeling is ridiculous but I don't care. "It's not my business to be glad, maybe, but I am. I am happy."

"Thank you, thank you Harry. You are sweet."

"No."

"But it was funny that you came back that way. Afraid that I would be angry."

"Weren't you? Before?"

"Yes, but you see, I knew that I was, I mean . . ."

"You knew about André when you were fighting with me?"

"Yes. So I have been sitting here hoping that you would come back, and not be angry with me, when you found out."

"I don't blame you Janine. How could I? I know how I acted. It was weak." And I cannot ask her why she did get so angry. Put me through that scene. "Now I could be angry with you. Because you didn't tell me first." She is trying to say something, but I know what it is. "No, don't, I know exactly what it was, and I feel exactly the same way. I just love you, I don't want it to be over, I am chagrined. I don't want to lose you, and only that thought makes me angry, and what you did is just what I half want to do now, just protest, because I can't bear to let this thing die quietly, it means too much to me. I would be ashamed to just leave, to let it go without saying something, and well . . ."

"Well, I was angry because I was jealous."

"Jealous. Jealous. Is that what you felt. You doll." Getting up holding my hands out to her. "Janine, you love," hug her and give her happy kisses finally.

"A little jealous. The other too. I felt you were being cool."

"Cool? Me?"

"Yes."

"I'm not cool."

"Yes you are. You were quite able to walk out and leave me without regret. You were so ready to run to Shirley."

"I am not cool to you, nor will I ever be. You have taught me a lesson."

"I don't think so."

"I do. I am very warm towards you. I felt so much for you that it bothered me. I knew it would be bad for you in the end."

"That is precisely what I mean. You could control yourself, you could still see, you knew what you thought you had to do."

"I don't understand." Still with our arms around each other talking so oddly this way. Close and yet far.

"You see when André and I talked earlier tonight, I didn't know what I was going to do. I didn't know for sure until you came back, until I suddenly realized what you thought there was between us, and then I realized, even while we were fighting. Not because of Shirley, but because of you. You see, Harry, you kept your head."

"Do you call this keeping my head?" Meaning our holding, our living here.

"This is only a beginning. You could not let it go more."

She is right. But is she saying, let's run away from them, or is she saying, we had the chance, and you did not take it, and so you do not love me? Or is she saying, you act, you only act, all I know is what you do, and therefore what is the truth about you? But she has given me the truth if I'll take it. "I guess I know what you mean, Janine." It feels like an admission. "But you see, it doesn't feel to me like being cool, what it feels like is this Don't run, Harry, stop somewhere, stand your ground, and face them."

"Face them? Face who?"

"The enemy. The squares. The guys who move the asparagus about."

Her uncomprehending look. Trying to explain and seeing the difficulty of her trying to understand.

"I see, Harry. That's what drove you from London."

"Yes."

But what I have told her is only a silhouette of what Shirley and I lived through. This is the real end for me.

And for the last time talking to Janine. The whole world is going to start changing tomorrow and I have to go out and meet it.

Never have I felt so useless. So many things to do. Not able to cope with this situation at all. Janine has gone, down there, and here I sit with the *Gazette* and coffee enjoying the hum of traffic far below this hung balcony looking over to the misty low green valley. Coffee after coffee and I sit here no longer allowed to practise my craft so long to learn.

Bloody tropics are getting to you again, there, Misfit. You should really get back to Blighty and the Missus and all the small Misfits. Never have I felt I fitted anywhere. That is supposed to bother you very badly, but I always knew I wouldn't. Comic, that. I mean, after all, the misfits of the world are the ones supposed to get the pity. Mispityfits. Missfits. It fits, Miss. Yes, apparently designed for you. Surely if monogamy were the intention, men and women would be monocoupled, like a series of cunning designs to prevent the lad from entering the wrong miss's doorway. But it's universally copulative, wherein our misfortune lies. Though to some a fortune it is in the little deaths they rehearse. The Summers theory of universal death wish as exemplified in the exhausting pursuit of the catchable.

For Christ's sake get up and to it man. The morning is not salted away but waits beneath the depressing dial.

The bleating bells of the space age in my telephone ear talking to Toronto. Hear the ruffle of pages turning four hundred miles away. Number and dial. Collect for Mr Michael Magee from Mr Ernest Hemingway in Montreal. Sounds of music in Mike's background.

Operator's May I have your name please sir?

"Sir Ernest Hemingway."

Her pause.

"We have a collect call for Mr Michael Magee from Mr Hemingway."

"Sir Ernest . . ."

"Will you accept the charges?"

"All right. Harry, that's on the three quid you already owe me."

"I'm sorry, Mike, I hadn't anything smaller than a hundred, and the phone in the Bugatti is broken, so I had to step out to this phone booth."

"I'm amazed you had the dime. And how come this is collect only from Montreal? Did you swim over?"

"Fantastic. I came by canoe. Listen, how come you have a phone? Are you respectable?"

"It's a front for my club. Do the police know where you are?"

"Mike. Good Lord. I'm hurt. Of course they don't."

"What are you doing here? Where's Shirl? This place is full of drunks. Come on over, it's a good party."

"You're four hundred miles away."

"Man this is only the second day. Come on. Did you sell the Morgan?"

My God, the car. At Shirl's. "Listen Mike, I left Shirl."

"Left her? You only just married her."

"It's a long story. Mike, give me some help. I need some names from you." But first this taradiddle from him about his new radio show. And working for TV. Ambitious Michael.

"Do you know any Separatists down there, Harry? I could use a good interview."

"Not a one, Mike. But I might get to some if it's important."

"Try to get to know a guy called René Châtelets. He used to work at the NFB. Get me an interview with that guy, and I'll do anything you like. He's supposed to be the head of some Separatist organization, and it could get me right onto THIS IS THE WEEK YOU LIVED.

"Okay. I'll do what I can. Now you get me this, please." And reading him from my last night's notes. Michael promising action. Reading off the number to him to call back. Mounts the bill as we go on talking, and yet again Mike is after me to do things for him, see people for him, round up interviews. Finally disentangling myself from his ambitions. Ask a Magee the time of day and you'll find you've just loaned him five hundred you had to borrow from somebody else. To pay him. He makes it seem as if you're paying him for being alive. Oh well Magee, you still owe me for your half of the bluefart Morgan and, when we sell it, I shall be amused to see you demand half what I get.

Tasks all done, homework shoved to the back of this thing I use instead of a mind. Now check again. Mike lined up, the names en route, noted safely to ask Janine re whatshisname for Mike, Langevin called and he to look out for Châtelets as well, and I to pick up the licence plates for the car. Buy vice grips to loosen the bolts on the existing plates, pick up a cheap summer suit to . . . phone again. Place is turning into an office. Mike perhaps?

But a cable from Shirl in London. Unfolding the terrible glad news. Read it back from memory to this kindly voice Arriving Air Canada Flight 857 Montreal Wednesday Love

Shirley. Crazy. Oh joy oh rapture unforeseen. Here at last to make it on our own.

Oh to jump from this verandah railing and sail over Montreal on joy. Actually coming. Her voice still a little in my ears agreeing, and now this glorious operator phoning me the cable, tomorrow flight 857. Arrangements to make and joy to live through waiting. God, it is a glorious morning out there in you city, below there, hear me? Shouting it aloud. "She's coming. Here, Montreal." Hah. More madness.

Down below to the ratholes where the people scurry in and out buying things for each other. Down to buy her somewhat in this odd little basement store which I have just viewed from far above. That. White with a scoopy fall to her bosom, and a train to the floor. Slippery looking thing. Fit her and hug her as I wish to do. Lucky dress so near those arounds. Now to this dreadful saleswoman actually seeming to smile at my discomfited pleasure. Remembering Shirley's size by how my arms go about her. A hundred and fifty. I'll take it. And to dress her with everything fresh and new from the epidermis out.

> *Singing in the morning, getting up for Shirl*
> *Going to go downtown and find that girl*
> *Today, this aft. tomorrow soon ...*
> *She's coming back by the light of the moon*
> *On a DC 8*
> *Really great.*

Can't stop humming *Water Music* and Mozart. The man was a sleigh bell. Going all the way downtown full of Shirley and Janine mixed. Yowsir. Into this laboratory of campy stuff where all canvas is shaped into thousands of interesting things. Such as this ideal Woods Downlite just right for summer evenings that zips together forming one bag large enough for not me and you poor unfortunate saleslady at this large store whom time has passed by leaving this red-washed hair looking motherly at me. Now bold Harry. "It's for our honeymoon." Do you think it is big enough to make love in? How the proper improper glance says what words do not. Portrait of a humped-up sleeping bag filled with Abide with Me fast falls the time away. "You see sir, you just spread it out this way and then zip." Struggling slightly. Mortification of the moonlit night unable to fit the male into the female zipper. "Like that. There. It's quite easy. Then you zip all round." Confusion of red plaid checked with black puffed inside over the guaranteed goosedown.

"I see. It's an excellent idea. Don't you think. Mm hm." But the price tag. It seems to say something. Impossible to read it with Shirley slipping into it that way. Just to turn my back now a little and tug away at the pink money belt. Pull it all out and pay. Embarrassment of having let her see all. Very stern with her now. Wrapping it in the bag and giving it to me in exchange for this wonderful paper that you can trade in on a night under the stars with Shirl.

"Thank you sir. I hope you find it satisfactory."

"Yes. I am sure we shall. Thank you." And now to hunt away for all the other gear. Paddle for Shirl. And paint her name on it in nail polish. Bottle of blue polish suitable for painting paddles, please. No blue. Then just this red will do nicely and thank you. Verso, Shirley, and recto, this amusing nude sketched as I walk about the large and humming empty store of a weekday morning with no one much about these lovely aisles full of what I want.

The Cabin

Behind the dotted glass, the passengers come out the far door insulated from us. There is one, coming to the counter now. Keep an eye on the door to see her. Now a couple more. Bags. The looking through. Insulated. People all round me waiting in groups and tears. Already in tears because someone has come. Part of this sobbing assembly. But to stand tall and not be affected. Christ my life is going to walk through that door any minute if she has come. Another group. She must be with them. No.

Coming out this door the first ones to emerge in Italian before Shirley has even made it to the. Her. No. Yes, it is in a light green dress looking around. Doesn't know where to go. Here. See me. Shirley. Wave. Embarrassed. She needs help. Let me in. She hasn't seen me. Can't wave again so soon. Why hasn't she seen me. Here, here. On my toes to be better seen. Waves. She saw me. Quick kiss in the air. Oh hurry girl. Standing in line with one bag in her green dress. Light green dress. How does she look there. Like Shirley. But strange. Tired? Afraid? Glad to see me. I hope she feels all right. Veuve Clicquot in the back seat to cheer her up. Standing in the line not moving much. Looks at me. Away. Keeps looking other places and then back to me. Smile. One smile, mine among all these people smiling.

At least she is down and safe, here and safe. The tedium of waiting while they look through her bag. Closed. Coming. Oh. Hurry. Not yet. Are you sure. Do I embrace her? Smiling through the door coming towards me head bobbing looking straight at me full of her. Shirley. Taking her bag.

"Shirley."

People standing back smiling. Little place among us here to take her in my arms and hug against the warm green dress. Her blue eyes. Such light in them. Sparks of light covering her.

"Hello."

"Hello." And standing with the bags unable to kiss.

"Was it a good trip?"

"Fine."

"I'm glad you flew."

Both smiling absurdly now, smiling as we exchange banalities. Not walking away. Something is undone. Left undone. Noise round us. Our little hole of quiet here. Shirley and I here, in this improbable aérogare, and it is all okay. Absolutely and perfectly all right now. She is here and I am here and it is all fine now. I can even lean over and give her this quiet kiss which turns suddenly into Italianate hug and murmuring to each other. Shirley Shirley Harry Harry and holding on smiling finally. Just holding and rocking her and here we are safe. Just hugging and no more words or thoughts in this gratitude. We made it. Even the beautiful plane didn't crash. Words later. Just pick up the bags and go and keep her close beside, smiling embarrassed catching each other looking. How tall I am walking banging into each other out the doors and over the edge to the car park and I hand her into Janine's car scarce able to bear parting smiling to go round the front anticipating the kiss again once we are inside. More conventional this time just holding and rocking in the front seat knowing it's done. Done and done. Can't even look at the dashboard for the sun in my eyes.

Helpless. How can I drive with you there looking so astonishing?

"Do we have to go anywhere?"

"No." Just to sit while the sun moves a little and the planes drop down and roar up again under the little clouds. So nice at last not to need to go anywhere. Just sit quietly holding on after all the threats.

"This is so nice, Shirl. So nice just sitting here. We don't have to go anywhere or do anything just sit here." With my arm round her and Shirl's head resting against me and neither of us needs to talk except for me needing to move the air round a bit. Her breath smells like apples. Her apple-scented breathing and wave of cloth in front of her for a little entertainment later. The real Shirley here. Incredible. This is the simplest moment of my life.

"I want to say something silly."

Not needing her mouthed assent.

"Me and thee."

Her mood accepts. "Forever and ever." No lifted head and shining eyes at my silliness. Just something Harry wanted to say. I can say anything to this lovely girl.

"You're lovely Shirl." A little vain hug for that. "Do you think I'll ever be able to drive with you so near? No, don't move."

"Can we go away somewhere?"

"Beautiful girl." Kissing her for that. To have my kisses accepted by that shining face. So agreeable. "You are a most agreeable girl, did you know that?"

"I guess so. Shall we go away somewhere?"

"Yes. Yes, I have a wonderful place. A cabin up on a lonely lake. Absolutely primitive. Canoes and oil lamps." My God, this is a very civilized English girl. Needs the Ritz. "Or else a posh hotel."

"The cabin, the cabin, Harry. It sounds just super. Can we go now? Where is it? How far? Will we be alone?"

"Absolutely and frighteningly. The only place on the lake."

"Oh, it sounds just beautiful. Is it far?"

"You mean you really want to go?"

"Oh yes, yes, yes. Now. Start the car." Bolt upright on the seat and eyes absolutely fastened to me.

"I thought you might be the least bit bored."

"No."

"Scared."

"No. Let's start. Oh, come on Harry. I've always wanted to do something like this."

"Not proper."

"I know." And her lovely deep hoarse laugh at that.

"Incredible laugh you get sometimes."

"Mother tries to stop me. Come on, Harry, start the car. I'm just dying to go."

"Well, all right." Curious. Never seen her like this. Madness of the Canadian summer. Full of light. Hah. And sweep this hard little sportsoh out of here and up the autoroute.

And we hit the autoroute at sixty and turn the trees past at ninety and hit these toll-barriers at twenty flinging in the quarters to the green péage baskets missing or laughing. In a Shirley-shilling too. No cops after us and turn right at this next one and plunge in east. Yes. A little slower now does it Harry as she turns to look back and see if Batman is after us.

Over our ancient inheritance on soft rubber, like Jews over the modern hills of Palestine on tank treads thinking of the horse-footed soldiers against Rome. At least we no longer wander.

"Do you like it?" Stopping by a brown stream like Coca Cola over brown rocks. Serenity and peace here by the sound of water.

"Yes. It's so bright and gloomy." Never commits herself.

"Gloomy?"

"Well the dark trees. And rock."

Then bowling greens with ladies in skirts. Last outpost. Shirley coming close. The scented kiss. Hair on my cheek. Beautiful burbling presence of a woman in my life like water in a dry country. The cranky little roads getting narrower and dustier. Verandahs hanging out from the ground floor like gaping toothless jaws on these old grey French houses. Narrow street winding through the town under maples.

"Everyone lives very close here."

"It's charming. I had no idea it would look so, old."

On a shaved hill in this harsh light, shadows. Hills in far shadow, and bright sunlight near. The heat.

"These big buildings on the hills – are they schools?"

"Monasteries, I think."

"They look so beautiful, and old. Like the Middle Ages one imagines." Her window open to get in some air and roll down mine to burn my arm in it. Sun and light on us. The smell of the woods getting closer round us. This is the wonder of my whole ruined life.

Climbing, gear down, pass the turn at the little town. St. Polycarpe. Was that the name? And on under the blue hydro towers to the final dirt track. Yes. Sight of the first lake's blue water there past the pines and round the corner slowly. Up the long dirt hill and down this abandoned trail. Yes. The dam there at the end. Nobody. Snap off the key and hear the after-silence of driving. André calling Allez-go and how we raced away down.

"This is it." Stretch out of the car and the bags in the trunk to the dirty edge of the landing in the failing heat. Breeze up the long river.

"What do we do now, Harry?" Her spiked shoes from the trans-Atlantic flight on this brown sand standing. A beautiful woman standing in a dress here alone. Who is with me.

"We portage."

Pick up the new red canoe and leave the old grey. Shirley's tall heels on the trail carrying one suitcase and the Woods pack clumsily. Too heavy for her straining in the heat. My expert roll of the canoe up onto my head unable to tell her that it is a hard thing to do as she watches me make it easy. And into the woods carrying heavy things one after the other with the mosquitoes on us and the sweat beginning to stand on us both in the heat.

At the landing fill up the swelling sides with Shirl's unsuited luggage and the good Woods pack with the leather straps looking so right in it and turn her about to face me so. She is just loving this and it suits me to face her with a paddle squeaking in my palms to make that island up the lake with the propane and musty beds in this warm late light all ours for as long as summer lasts. Round the swimming reefs, down the lake with the north wind pushing fast at us, and carefully land. Not spilling Shirley. Show her up the dangerous path to the cabin clearing, and the swimming log. Our own island in its perfect hour.

"That's west," pointing for Shirl taking off her shoe with a show of slip on the swimming log. Sitting at home on the log. Warm light on us and shadows beginning to mean something on the rock.

Unbelievably here. With her.

"Let's swim."

"All right." Picking up the bag to go up to the cabin.

"No."

Taking off my shirt moneybelt and looking at her. My shoes off. Water flat and looking at her. My voice strong.

"Shouldn't I change?"

"There's nobody around. Come on." And Shirley in the light undoing her green dress and laying it on the rock. Marvellous. Stockings. Full up slip. Last little things and her all exposed to the moving air. For the moth wind to blow over her in the light. Bare feet on the rock to the edge and hold her hand. Let the brown water come over us and wash away our past. Judaic. Gone in a moment and baptized in the new world. The water intimate with her playing between her English legs and rolling over her bosom. And to silently emerge thus in the light wet scarcely looking about for a towel. Embarrassed to stand heading for the log to sit and our wet bottoms beside on the dry log soaking us up. Arm around her and still sitting watching the light. To say it was a lovely swim? To say May we? Make love? Turn and kiss her again and look in her wide-set and blue eyes quietly looking at me without recourse and ending by holding her skin close in these little sounds we make.

Hasty looking about for something to lie on needless in the summertime. But just beside her lie down and we are all that is alive on this infertile rock. Still she looks at me and knows and does not say. It is all right. It is permitted and I want to now, clumsily trying not to pain her. Only us warm and soft on the hard back of the earth. Me atop you in this amazing position. Head between my hands saying I love you, you are beautiful. Over and over beautiful I love you dying and I love you live. Must get it right and no second chances. But in there somewhere I am sure. Awkward pain. Can't be right. Toes on rock. Slip slip. Elbows. Not hurt you. Just whatever it is. Gone. Gone and gone. Everything gone. Have I done it right? What do I do now? Kiss and love. In her ear. Love you again. Beautiful softness of your hair darling. So lots of it massy sliding to kiss and mingle in my hands.

"You're hurting . . . there." Moves me.

"I'm sorry dear." Up on my hands looking down.

"That's nice." Smiling up at me from down there all eyes and lips and hair about her head lying on the rock and bosom sitting visible. Running her hands up and down my back and smiling. As if I have done it right.

"You were just a bit heavy."

"With love." And now more expertly without weighting her lean down to kiss her lips open with my head slightly aslant. And up again just brushing her up and down the length of her with my long weight. This is very fine. Can I ask her how it was and if I did it right? But no, still embarrassed to talk about us in the midst of it and sort of slink quickly into the water without looking and stand water-clothed on the rocks neck deep looking over the smooth silk between us solemnly. Laughing. Able to say over this slight separation I love you easily and no qualms. Her smile and smile goes on.

What passes for happiness now looks at me from the face of an English girl. Saying it to her. How silent she is. Speaks with her face. Ye gods, as she gets hippily barebacked out of the water again I want her again. Dare say it? I am not sure I even had her just now. Just the first time. Lots of time to practise. For all I know I had it in the wrong spot. Conceivable I was bunting away between her legs and didn't hit anything vital. Impossible. How dare I ask her? Or ask her help next time. Damn silly just to get up there and bunt like that. Might have hurt her. Still in the water abashed at this repeating sign of my fidelity already rising again. Not to get out of the water yet while she has found a towel and starts to dry herself. Throws it to me nicely so I can emerge and not be seen. But suddenly being seen anyway not caring because what the hell. I have been on top of you and said I love you, you are beautiful and all I want and I have held your head between my hands as I towel away desiring you more and more.

"See what I mean?"

"Yes. Beautiful. And so quiet. All round."

Will she think me a beast if I start it again? I am a beast. Of love. "Yes. Beautiful."

"Are there many places like this in Canada?" Not with you naked towelling away.

"Half the country is like this. Nobody. Don't get dressed." Is dressed. Did she hear me? Did it even happen?

"Aren't we lucky?" For what, Shirley? Am I yours?

Moving through the cabin unable to think of anything else. Seeing the stove and stone fireplace and the bed. Where it lies behind the wall of my imagination. Having our first dinner together beside the cabin window with the table pushed over so we can watch each other watch the evening stretch out calmly over the water and breathe. The day relaxing and going to sleep in the slow darkness. Quiet and peaceful in here listening to the crickets and the looncall.

What month can this be? Is there much summer left?

"I wish we could stay here forever."

"It must get very cold in the winter."

Watching her move prettily about these years of days later in what must be the ritual of woman. It does not seem complicated, but the undoing and the stepping, the unfeeling of the back turned or not, the bashfulness or not, is in me is in her as we must undress to the moon window and throw our shadows on the broad bed before we lie down. And what is she saying now as she comes over close to me and speaks not into my ear where I must whisper things in the midst of love, but aloud almost to the ceiling as if she were talking to herself and I inside her to listen as well.

"I'm so glad I came. It's just what I wanted." To turn and slowly run her hand over my face.

"Are you happy?"

"Yes."

And she feels no more to say. Just looks at me and I do not feel my face shows happiness. But fear. Thought. Can it last? Is it even now? All I have ever had. Ever likely to have. She is so innocent. Like china to be broken. And I must not break that look.

Lies her head down looking at my look and goes to sleep. Lying and wondering about this cabin in the dark beside the still lake and her beside me breathing. And she is already asleep lightly beside me not moving. Face closed. Moon over the lake. No more birds or night birds. Faint cool pressure of air slipping down the hill towards the lake, the night's cool wind. Slip out of bed not to disturb her and feel it on me. Only a few nights like this in a year. Leaf rustle here or there once or twice. Alone in the night with the moon going by. Something. Thought. These days have been. Write. And at the table set it down for her in the morning. Poem to greet you in the morning.

To sit up and look through the shady screen to the day. Wind tearing through the pines. Plane going over. How to get up without being seen. Bad enough to have this absurd figure of mine with the short legs covered in blond hair, but to bulge the

139

pyjamas also with this early morning sensation is too much. Nor do I wish to turn upon her just now. She is getting familiar after these many mornings and we still have not talked. But I must give her some kind of kiss. Just lean over in the bag hidden from the hips down and kiss her round forehead. How she watches me with her eyes. Fastened to me. They move as I move about the room. Faithful. "Good morning dear. You are very beautiful." And now she moves in the bed comfortably. Quick get up and out.

Out the back door to sniff the air and not look below. Just stand in the bush barefoot letting it happen below unattached to me and keep my eyes on the trees above. Are you getting me into deep trouble, old boy? Prodding about first while all is unresolved?

But down to the shore and pull off the pyjamas and plunge in for a shiner. And swim about gently, under a couple of times and out into the sun. Run up for a towel pretending you are at camp again, or at the cottage with mum and dad and all is well and very young again. You are okay and safe.

Into the room familiarly for the towel and sight of her just doing up this and that. She is all globes and long smoothness, paint her in curves unending, flowing all together and rippling out again there and here. A decoration on that point and one to match on the other. Full pale fall and shadow curving below. And that shield below of curves pricked with light. This soft thing can't hurt you. Just walk up and palm her this way and belly up close kissing her with your mouth sweetened by the fresh water and taste her wide kiss first thing in the morning making the day. And a hand or two down her glorious back to the place where she swells. She swells all over.

"All I can think of to say is super and dull things, Shirl. Like good morning. What a nice way to wake up." She likes to press her cheek against my bare shoulderchest. I guess she likes comfort too. Just give her a little and don't be mean, you selfish lout. Just let her have what she wants. Large-sized squeeze with her arms about my chest. Standing here both barefooted enjoying it. What has happened to her reluctance, and the May knickers. Don't ask yet. Just take it all in.

"It's a sin to get dressed."

"Well let's have breakfast. I'm hungry."

The poem. Quick put a flower beside it for her to see. Something blue down by the water. Yes. Run down and snap it off and into an orange-juice glass and beside her place. Potter about the woodstove bringing it to the boil in this fresh air with the window open and the light onto the wood table. And she sees it. Up. Reads. Oh not aloud Shirl. It's no good. It's only from me to you.

These years of days
Are yours and mine
And hours we live
Like clocks of flowers
Turning with the sun.

These days like years
Are water idylls
*   Mountains sharp with love*
*   My moving light and rain*
*   All over you.*

Turning with the biggest smile.

"What is it? Is it anything Shirl?"

"I like it Harry. It's beautiful. Thank you." Standing foolish having done something pretty and absurd.

"It sort of makes you feel sharper to me." But at least she isn't sentimental about it. Just likes it and sets it down beside as we eat. And there it is my missive from the night not even having spelled idyll right I bet. Actual tiny poem bursts out of me like an unexpected wink. And plot the day after this little beginning picnic.

First to the unpoetic dishes which are acceptable looking out the many-barred old glass windows over the green-iron kitchen hand-pump. A buzzing fly or two in the woodscented

141

heat. I bring you water in the old galvanized pail to do the dishes and we stand inside with all the windows flapped up on rusty hookeyes smelling the morning air where the white sink disgorges outside to the pine needles staining the rock and wipe and dry and put away without worrying. And there was a prickle of rain on the dry roof-eaves here last night. Quietly while we slept. Beautiful. Why the forest smells today. To sing. Holy Holy Holy. Casting down their golden crowns around the glassy sea. Time like an ever rolling stream. My awful voice and Shirley joining in makes me sing better. She sings, she is unassuming, she is beautiful, she likes this cabin, she came all the way across the Atlantic on the damnedest dare, she hasn't even mentioned the awful things I do, she wants no confession, she even seems to like me, and she wants to stay here regardless of all. What we are unable to say, what we have not said in these days weeks yet does not seem to matter to her. I love her. I love her.

Put the towel aside and come up behind her and arms round the little waist. Lifts her elbows to let me round and leans back against me.

"I love you Shirl. I love you and love you." Easy to say to the back of her neck. I know she is looking out the window as I say all this and she is sharply seeing the blue sky through the pine needles above and accepting it all. A beautiful place and early morning time to say it.

Symbolic to go out in the canoe in the bright air smelling the hot dust of rocks and the pine trees. Shirley backed against the forward thwart looking towards me, not at me, but towards me. Pretty band in her hair all that these Solomon's eyes need.

"Is there a flower called Solomon's Eyes, Shirl?"

"Solomon's Seal."

"I shall paint one and name it Shirley's Eyes. An utterly new flower. From my own hand." She looks around, not quite smiling. My own hand. What have I said. Did that bother you?

"What is it Shirl?"

"Nothing."

"What nothing?"

"Nothing, Harry. Really."

But there was something in her eyes. What did I say to start it off. Something from my own hand. The ring. Not the wedding ceremony. For the few bits of news we have exchanged in these couple of days, talking about life in London long ago, about Montreal and André and Janine, who is carefully edited away out of my conscience, because I am all ease now, what for all that, have we said about that terrible night. When I ran away.

I know what it was. The ring, the ring is bothering her.

"Was it about the ring, Shirl? Don't hide from me. I can't stand that. Please."

"I thought how hurt you must have been."

"I wasn't hurt. Or, perhaps I was. But that was the thing that got me in the end. It was the symbol you see."

"I thought so, when I heard about it."

"And I couldn't tell you, because I felt it was the beginning of what in fact did happen."

"I know. Now, I know. But why didn't you tell me at the time?"

Paddling remotely trying to understand why I didn't. "For that reason really. I saw the crack in the façade of that wedding. You and I had agreed that we wouldn't spend anything on a ring. You remember. Waste of money, and besides a sign of bourgeois decadence or something. Then when your father turned up with it, and gave it to me, with signs of perfect pleasure, I knew that was the end. But of course, at that stage, I was afraid to admit it. The consequences were ferocious, so I just gave you the ring and told you I'd sold a painting. Shirley, I was ashamed I had to do it."

"Harry. Oh, Harry."

"But it wasn't just that, Shirl. It was my being unable to resist that first reaching-in trying to shape what we had to be, and how we were to live and act. I knew by instinct then, but I didn't know entirely till that night. The last night."

Now her uncanny ability to sit quiet through something like this that tears my guts out, threatening everything in me.

I seem to be forcing this upon her which perhaps she does not want. What does she want from me? What will it be? But keep on Harry. It hasn't all been said.

"Then when you were so sort of accepting about it all, I was bewildered. That last night."

"Why?"

"I didn't seem to be getting through to you."

"You were."

"I have your word. Now." A flat statement which she accepts.

"You don't believe in vows, Harry. You don't make them."

"I know." And that says it. But what. Is this all, between us? These few days in a cabin. She seemed to want so much more before and now, nothing. Just to be, like this.

Able to paddle round the bend telling her a few things as we go. To a cliff she likes and hang under it smooth in the water in the darkness. Looking out of darkness to the beach over there. Or is that far gold line rock near the water? We slide over to see and near it, a stream coming down from some distant field, some distant grassy lake. Paddling slowly by the creek mouth looking at the withered grey logs along the shore edge. A beaver swimming by so near we can see him under the water grey-black shape, long oval tail. Telling her about the house and dam, the exploding dynamite against the flooded highways. Talking only a little as we go along on the lake. A beautiful curving lake with many bays and inlets, islands at the far end there according to the topsheet in the cabin. And Shirley has suddenly begun talking. London, the wedding, mother. Listening back as I go now quite slowly paddling to the point over there looking low and flat with a bit of brightness showing through promising a level spot out of this sun bouncing up too hotly now where we can land and stroll up into the pines. Face of her mother looking at me over her shoulder in the far green trees – how brilliant the image of my London town. She was very disappointed in me, felt I had much to offer, could have done so well in London and all the friends liked me.

"That's new."

"They like you Harry." In the present.

"Why?" Makes me feel sullen. Bunch of old boots.

"I knew you weren't happy. I tried to explain it to her, but mother is very old-fashioned. She thinks men should come home every night and listen." She laughs and I can see her thinking "Mother." How separate she is now. Always has been, Harry. No, not now.

"I think that's what I like in you best, Shirley."

"What?" You see, she doesn't know. Not to tell, in her style. And her easily waiting for me to tell. Just to paddle and not tell, for once. But she invites me to, by not asking.

"It's maddening, the way you don't ask."

"Do tell." Leans.

"Bitch."

"Please tell Harry." Smiling.

"Can't remember. What was it?" With you so independently there in my power, damned attractiveness of you. "Your attractiveness. Threatens me. You take me, all my independence, and will never lose your own. Constant battle for ascendancy. You never win because you never battle." Flick of paddle water in her pale blue English unsuitable blouse to ruffle her.

"Child."

"Now you know."

"That's not what you were going to tell me."

"Why should I tell all, and you nowt?"

"Because you want to. Besides, I have nothing to tell."

"I couldn't reach you Shirl. That's why I ran away. I couldn't reach you. I felt you did not understand, and that's why it took me so long to call you, and get you over."

"Long?"

"Weeks."

"I didn't think you could get settled any sooner."

"Oh."

"Were you delaying?" How gently she asks that.

"I felt that after that last night, it might have been over."

"What do you mean? If I'd known that, I'd never have let you go. Alone."

"I meant, that what I felt when your father forced the engagement ring on us, was the first crack, the sign, and that the night at the party, at Nigel's might have been a similar sign that, well . . . never mind . . . it's over." This is terrible. Too hot here. Get out of the beating sun. Afraid to look at Shirl for what I have suddenly guiltily brought into this brilliant scene. Where all was love and peace. Oh damn me. This spurious honesty.

Get up the rock wondering what she is thinking. Slant the canoe out of the water as Shirl stands there. Unable to look at her.

Follows me up the needles here in the dark woods to sit down. This is the truth, first time. She sits on a log in shorts and her delicate legs are partly lit by the gold sun. A slanting line from her left thigh down to her right ankle in the sun's angle. Looks at me for more.

"I had no idea you felt that way."

"What else could I think, when you couldn't say you would come?" Looking dismally down at the ground.

"You might have told me." She's reaching for you Harry. Don't go.

"You might have known."

"How?" Her pain, but dammit. "If we had loved each other, you would have known."

"That's what you always say. But I love you. I felt for you. I thought you were afraid, I wanted to help."

"Huh."

"I was afraid I'd lose you, and you knew it. You did, Harry." She looks angry.

"I knew I had to get out."

"Why didn't you say so?"

"I did, I tried to, I thought I was."

"But you only said you had to get away from my family, from London, the whole scene. The way you got away from Canada."

"Yes, Shirley, I did, I know I did, but when I saw your re-

146 / The Lonely Ones

action, I suspected you didn't care enough to come then. Love acts on impulse, I guess."

"But that's only a difference between you and me, between two temperaments. It didn't mean I didn't love you. I said I did, then, and I would come with you."

"Yes, but I was afraid of the sign, the first break between us, you see, and you being able to let me go."

"That isn't . . ."

"I know – I know." And realizing stupidly, dully, that love is not clinging, but letting go too. Letting go because you love. Even as she says it. Harry, you didn't know.

"It wasn't even that I let you go, Harry. It was because you said that was what you had to do, what you wanted to do, so I agreed. You know I did."

"Yes."

"I didn't *let* you go. I didn't feel I *had* you. Still, sometimes, I don't."

"I was reaching for it from you, that's all. I wanted you to be eager for me, I felt you didn't show me you loved me. I've always been afraid you didn't love me, that you were just reacting. I'm still afraid of that." And how can she accept that sitting in the wilderness with this Canadian not knowing what is next? "I'm sorry Shirl." She is getting ready to cry.

"You see I've always felt I didn't show it enough." How she is whispering out of pain. "Never showed anybody enough. I've always known that was what was wrong with me. Making a failure of me."

"Don't cry." Can't bear to have caused it in her. "It's over now. I was afraid but I'm not now, Shirl. Believe me, it's over, and I love you and take it easy, please. I didn't mean to hurt you like this, I didn't even know I could," and looking in my eyes she knows that I wanted to see if I could hurt. Do you love me enough to suffer? "Christ, I'm sorry. It was a dismal thing to say now." Just sitting waiting for something to happen. Sneak a look or two at her beside me on the log looking aftermath still pained. Not holding onto it as I do but it draining away from her face leaving her looking soft and hot, eyes huge and filmy. Like warm fruit, spoiling. How does she feel? Resentful?

"Please, I'm sorry, Shirl." And now two burnt-out cases sitting in the woods unable to touch. "It's just that I guess I didn't understand you very well, till now."

"What I don't understand about you, Harry, is that you accuse me of silence, of repression and inhibition, and not saying I love you, and not giving signs and not holding on . . . when all along you have been acting the same way, and not telling me what you thought and felt but just leaving, when you thought it was the end."

"I didn't say I thought it was, I said I was afraid it might be . . ."

"Isn't that the same thing. Or worse."

"I don't know."

"And how could you say you were still afraid I didn't love you after . . . oh I don't know."

"I didn't understand, Shirl. Not entirely. I do now."

"You're worse, because you can say these things so much better than I can."

"All I can say is, I know better now."

"I hope you do."

And walking away neither together nor apart. Down to the canoe. Stand here for a moment remembering this place. Afraid of it.

How does she react? Is she leaving? Is it over? What do we do hanging about the cabin now, spoiled for each other by the storm? I have lost something to her, and we must discuss returning.

"Are there any galleries in Montreal?"

"Dozens. Why?"

"I was thinking of getting a job." She talks as she works round the table setting.

"I still have some money. I've paid the rent on the new flat for two months." Does she take that in? Are we going to live together, or have I broken it all up? To begin to pack only half discussing whether or not we go. But I cannot say "shall we live together?" And after the first fiasco to suggest a wedding is absurd. We walk in the room together putting things away and vaguely talking of coming back. It is okay to cohabit here, but what about town, where people will know. Perhaps that is what she means as we walk down to the canoe putting things in. Locking the door on the past here and I cannot stay silent and I cannot speak. Walking down. In sadness, paddling away. The wrong way to leave.

But at the landing where something must happen before we actually leave this spread beauty to its silence and dark nights and long winter light I have to have this emotional scene ashamed of myself and so making it stiff in my mouth as I say it.

"Shirley," scarcely looking at her, "shall we live together or what?" Must have it in words. What can she say? Amazing laughter.

Standing on the landing looking at me as if I didn't know myself. And her laughter makes me laugh. To stand a moment outside myself laughing looking in at the dark fear and doubt of that suddenly slope-shouldered figure of me on the landing afraid of himself. Laughing at it.

It is easy driving back from the lake in this country so like mine, and not quite my own, to start telling her about it all. I crave this beauty. Lucky to be in it. And suddenly the mixture of what it means to me together with what it means to André. Where he started painting, right around here.

Talking it all out for Shirley how Port Faith was glorious in those fall days, all blue and gold over the blue streets and the steep hill falling always to the river at your knees boiling with the ice of spring and the smelts running where you could pick them out with the kitchen sieve. Where the far lake thrashed under the south storms driving the sand back into the cliffs eating the ground from under your bed at night and hearing

149

the freighters hoot past the lighthouse in your warm window. The moon on their decks. Then sliding along molten on a summer night five miles out on the stillness hearing their frog-croak voices and their decks clang with the ring of iron feet. Light shine walking on a thousand stilts over the black floor of the sky. Mysterious sliding city lights travelling the worn compass line down the international lake to the submarine sea.

Apple-voiced women in old kitchens talking in their long-distance aprons through the black wall hollow to pies baking on Brock Street that went on cooking in the oven for the mysterious network of grown-ups missing Daddy at the war. My mother's craggy face turning sour turning bright again with the lines beginning to henpeck her fine skin. Of Gana-raska and Muskoka born am I, and bitten from an Ontario Macintosh apple in the snapping fall. I should go back there and fructify; I am no good at revolution.

"I'm rambling." Shirley having listened.

"Yes."

"I feel it's going to be bad."

Shirley nodding. "How did André get you into this raid?"

"He didn't. Or else . . . I don't know. I felt I owed it to him. He did so much for me, in Paris. I said I would take his studio here, to front for him, and we talked about the Separatists, and I don't know, I felt I owed him something for the past. As if I owed him something. Your kind did him in Shirl, and now we have to pay for it."

"Did him in? What do you mean? Wolfe at Quebec? That's ancient history."

"Yeah. It is. No, I mean, simply, we disregarded them, and they were next door. They had a problem and we walked by. Now suddenly we realize we are getting a message from some guy who is on the other side right now, you hear him talk, you see his face showing what you don't want to see, what is painful to see – abandonment, need, tremendous solitude, so bad he can't say it all, and all of a sudden you remember something – oh you know what it is like to be alone on a lake up north, nothing but trees, and see a canoe suddenly appearing far away. Man, you wave. You wave to him, and he waves back. That's all this is. Well the strange thing about this big lonely country is, you didn't wave. Something told you not to, somebody bigger and older and smarter. French or English, it didn't matter, they were all the same. So. Now we're waving. And maybe it's too late."

the
lonely
ones

Montreal

She comes into this room like morning light and looks at me and says ever so lightly, "It's warm out. I think it may rain later." And turns. And walks to the window. Incapable of malice. All English softness. To relax and look at her pritter about this place gently. Tentative way she holds out her arms to me to get me up but I lie here just so I can watch her little performance which she slowly becomes aware of making as she sits down beside the window with the light falling upon her and lying on her shoulder like an award. For conspicuous beauty.

"We have several unpleasant facts to face, Shirley."

"I know. Why do you wear a moneybelt?"

Solemnly taking it off. Embarrassment taking it off that time in the middle of love making when it was cold on her. Drop it over the edge of the bed.

"I think I'll have to give it up, Shirl. I can't figure whether to wash it, dryclean it or just get it polished."

"I thought at first it was some kind of Canadian girdle."

"I guess it is." Sadly hang it over the fencepost here. "There's an empty saddle in the old corral tonight." Remarkable how the zipper never once jammed. "Damned good moneybelt, that. Symbol of my roving past. Maybe it's a symbol of my latent homosexuality."

"Hah."

"Rude noise. It could be, Shirl, you know. Sort of masculine chastity belt making love-making too embarrassing."

"I haven't noticed it stopping you."

"No. Of course, you wouldn't."

"Well, what shall we do?"

"Face the unpleasant facts. Money, marriage, job, parent. The whole bit. And André. I promised him . . . I have to call Janine."

And explaining yet another of my embarrassments to Shirl as she uncomprehending tries to realize this strange business of taking André to the radio station. Fronting for the patriots. All while we get dressed in wifely fashion strapping on all the strange underthings one after the other. "The female steeplechase course."

"What do you mean, steeplechase?"

"Each a little challenge. Fence or hedge to hurdle before you reach the finish line. Here."

And boldly my palm cups her. How strange that it is now permitted. Sweet Shirl. A matutinal kiss for you dear.

"Aren't you going to tell me to behave?"

"No. Why should I?"

"Life is real and life is earnest and the goal is to behave."

"No. Besides, you overestimate my upbringing. My inhibitions hadn't a hope when I met you."

"Liar."

"Well." And that huge smile I am coming to love. Making me feel entirely weak. How her face rounds and fills with enormous smiles. How she does not know that a smile is a gamble. The smile given is pain risked.

"Your smile devastates me. Inside."

"Good." And rounds it up again and gives it to me. What lovely significance is in it. I love you.

"Shall we?"

"What?"

"Go down and phone."

"I know you meant something else."

"I know. I always do. But we have unpleasant facts to face this morning. And I do have to call."

"Okay."

It is absurd to go arm in arm out of this crummy flat down these ratty dark stairs which are too narrow for it but we do, pressed together by the narrow walls whose single advantage is knocking us pleasantly hip to hip .

"We must get married Shirl."

"We will. We virtually are."

"How do you know?"

"You've taken off your precious moneybelt."

"Hm." A quizzical look at her in the dim dark stairwell. "You know me too well already." Only a small smile now, but she does not cling to me. Just is pleasantly beside. Harry, you lucky oaf, you have landed on your claws once again after vast tribulations. You shall overcome. I wish I could kiss her again and say I love you again but it is getting kind of boring. Perhaps love is measured by the number of times you need not utter it.

And on Mrs. Lombard's old hall wall phone getting Janine. The two girls talking, exchanging their womanly news until I can get back on and efficiently arrange the meeting for this afternoon until we go tonight. A La Crêpe Bretonne. Harry to get the car and prepare to drive them to the station after a French blintz. Which gives Shirl and me still a couple of hours to wander about downtown showing her this old city.

"Well, how would you like some pancakes?"

"All right. Where?"

"There's a little crêperie downtown full of phony atmosphere for the tourists, which the French infest so heavily that the tourists can't get in. It's jammed with Separatists protesting the inherent phoniness of North American civilization. And the food is superb. Shall we?" Out the long hall with a bow to Mme. L. and to walk downtown with my girl this day.

Actually becoming respectable. Respectable in daylight are Shirl and Harry.

"We have a few hours to kill, Shirl. What would you like to do first?"

And now to follow her girlish whims as she takes me to an antique shop, and the gallery with the Moore in front, and bags of peanuts watching Le Bonheur. Oh to be out of school like this with Shirl enjoying the daytime world. It can't last Harry. It is too nice to walk into a store this way with some money to spend, and to spend it on an unnecessary blue sweater for Shirl to model so I can cast a critical eye on the line and colour, savouring the front jut of her youth. The mood is high. We walk seeing all and sometimes seeing nothing sitting with a beer outdoors across from good old McGill pointing out the fraternity house and where one got drunk mainly with shouts and meeting new people in the exciting days when you were far from home here playing fast and loose on two beers after the game. Life is better when you haven't got your home-work done.

Finally to Crêpe Bretonne in time. In the half dark from the sunny street searching for Janine on the hard bench past the brick cookery. We meet. Thunderous insignificance of our parrying hellos. Too tense, too tense to be friends of a sudden. Janine begins to sketch it in and now I am responsible.

"Everything is fine, Harry. There is only one change. You are to drive my car to the rally, that is, my sister's car. You wait just inside the front entrance as André showed you. . . ."

"Wait a minute, he didn't show me. The place was closed when we went by."

"Oh." Her right hand across her chest to her left shoulder. Plucking. Nervous.

"Does it matter, Janine, it seems an ordinary place. Have you been in it?"

"No. He wanted everything precise. I don't know what to do." The silence. People next table talking too loud. Can't think. "Are you coming, Janine?"

"Yes."

"Why?"

"André said it would be good to have girls in the car at the radio station. It would look natural. Reassure the commissionaire.

"Is there room?"

"We can squeeze in."

"Well the layout must be simple. Anyway, it's too late unless we can get in touch with André now."

"No."

"Well, we just go to the door at the hall and look round. The three of us will be there."

"Yes, I'm sure between the three of us we'll see him."

"And anyway, Langevin will be there."

"Yes, I was nervous, things have been happening so fast around here. I'm sure it will be okay."

"I'll be back in a minute." Shirl going off to the washroom. Leaving us suddenly alone.

"We're going back to the cabin afterwards, Harry."

"Yes, I know."

"All of us."

"He knows Shirley is here."

"Yes."

The silence coming in over us.

"We've just come from there."

"Yes. He wants us to get away somewhere completely remote. Montreal will be too dangerous for a while."

"Yes, I've been thinking about that. But it will be difficult. Did he mention Shirley and me?"

And she returns as I mention her name. Janine's nerves are pulled like piano wires. "How long have you been in Montreal, Shirley?"

"Didn't you know? I came over three weeks ago."

"Oh, yes."

"We were at the cabin till yesterday. Then we came down."

"Oh, I didn't know." Silence. Of course you knew Janine. You lent me the car. "It was beautiful up there, Janine." Haven't I just said that? To feel that it is a faux pas talking of my happiness in front of Janine. My situation is terribly mixed.

"I'm sorry, I'm so distracted. I have to think of so many things. The car is outside, Harry. Here are the keys. Again."

"You're not leaving."

"No, but you're supposed to drive, aren't you?"

"Oh yes, that's right." Now she's getting me nervous. We'd better get out of here. It's almost time. This is either a moment of tiny greatness beginning. Or totally fatuous. Now Janine gets up. Are we going too soon? Another few minutes are left. But we walk out. Expecting every moment the sirens out Ste. Catherine to Pie Neuf and up to Honfleur, right and into the summery darkness along this old street. Many cars about as we search for a place to leave this old Mustang. At last up the sidestreet under the summer shining night trees. To approach this hall's broad old portico in Graeco-Roman style with the overheavy pediment. Tall pillars, of entesis not too proud but nicely shading the porch where so many Liberals are gathered within. The Prime Minister. Quietly listening. A warm night and all are listening to the world inside, the speakers' words broadcast outside here to cops in uniform lazily standing by squad cars but their sharp eyes rove us as we approach. Fun to ask them which way to André but I sense Janine dragging me past them with her even as we go. And together with Shirley we enter to smoke and noise and crowded shoulders pressed together, heads back looking up over other heads demanding to see the speakers through the acres of smoke up towards the front. Seats filled with people ahead of this crowd standing at the back as the loudspeakers bleat at us in French. How I scarcely notice which language it no longer is. If afterwards someone asked me which language it was said to me in, I wouldn't know unless I thought. As André and I switch back and forth, and these speakers do tonight as well. Surely there is hope for such a nation of linguists.

Nice to have Janine holding onto my arm here. But overly suggestive.

"We're supposed to meet back here, Janine. But I don't see him."

"Neither do I."

"Why don't you go up that side, and I'll go up here, and we'll meet back here in three minutes."

"Okay." But too many people, can't move properly. Noise of the huge mechanical loudspeakers braying too loud and harsh at us. Damned annoyance of having to shout at each other while the voices so loud. How can anyone hear anything in this noise. Hey, there's André.

"Shirley, Shirley, this way." And pulling her through and round these shirted backs.

"Where's Janine?"

Where is he running? Why running? I'm on the floor. I've fallen. What happened? Noise, huge explosion. Airblast. People. Shouts. People all round too close. Get up, get up. Explosion. A bomb.

"Shirley." Getting her up. "Are you all right?"

"What?"

"Bomb." Another tremendous bang. Oh Jesus. Air blast. People shout.

"Shirley, they're throwing bombs. Get out." Grabbing her hand and back towards the door. Insane shouting here. Shove that idiot. "Come on, allez-go." Push out. The door. Luckily near entrance here. Not yet in. It's a riot. This is a riot. Get Shirl by pillar here and stop. People all surging out and one man carrying a dog to his chin walking unconcerned for self and saving dog as all the others run by him in French look at them go running and running to street. These incredible people now standing clustered round the doors awaiting more bombs. Oh André, come.

"I see him, Harry. I see him." And Shirley has found him. With Janine. Over there. Stand tiptoe and scream to him. "André, André, ici, ici. . . ." Push over to him. Something wrong with him. What's happened.

"Come on Harry, lead us."

And just as fast as I can and get to the car. Along the

street and across and up. A decent touch of darkness here for our dark deed. But all over your back André, mosquitoes. Mosquitoes' blood.

By the car. "Here it is, André. My God, you're bleeding. You're hurt." All over his back, shirt torn skin ripped blood coming out. Bone.

"You've got to get to a hospital."

"It feels. It feels not too bad." Suddenly closing his eyes and leaning over the hood. Streetlight in this tree beside spotted shadow on him. People running, talking, standing. Can't see. Matches. If I smoked. "Janine, you smoke, some matches." Snapping the lighter to it. Carefully take off the torn jacket.

"Here, my shirt, Janine." Pull it off and how do you bandage a back?

"How does it look?"

"Hard to say. There's some blood all right. Do you feel pain?"

"Yes. It burns. Badly now."

"Look, I'll put my shirt over it so you won't get dirt in it."

"We must get to the station, Harry."

"We can't. Not now." Collaring the shirt round his neck with Janine and gently draping it down. Noises behind. We must go.

"André you'll have to get into the car like this. Janine, shove the front seat forward and get in beside. There. Now hop in old man. Take it easy."

"It's not too bad. I'm all right."

"In we get. Hold your arm there, Janine. Yes. That's it."

"Okay Harry." Quiet look on her face. Pulling off her jacket to stuff behind his neck and hold him forward.

Start and gently go. "Where's the nearest hospital?"

"Harry, I'm not going. We must get to the station."

"Hey, there's Langevin." Pull up beside him carefully in the swirling mob and lean out the window. "André's been hurt. We have to get him to hospital. We can't go to the station."

"What happened? Do you know? I heard an explosion.

Look, they're sending up ambulances." And the wail in the night past us.

"We have to get out of here, Langevin. I don't know what happened."

"It was a bomb, I'm sure."

"I'm taking André to the hospital."

"But Harry, what will we do?"

"Get out, I guess. We never planned for this. I don't know."

"André?" Leaning through the window. André hardly able to speak telling us to go on.

"He can't breathe properly, Langevin. We must go."

"Yes. We'll cancel the station. For now. Another night, perhaps." And looking at him, both knowing this is the night.

"Yes. Pierre is in my car. I'll tell him. Follow me to the hospital."

"Okay."

And weaving down through the city night apparently peaceable in this part nearing centre of town. Slowly not to jar André and keep Langevin's old blue Chev in line ahead. Here. He stops. Another ambulance. But from where?

"We wait here. Langevin will tell us." And just to wait breathing in this atmosphere. Same hectic feeling tonight as of sudden celebration. Here he comes.

"Harry, you must get away, right now." Leaning close. "I saw police there. All over the place. I don't know why they are there. A lot of people hurt, I guess. But I think it is too dangerous." The great hulk of the rescuing hospital standing over the midtown street unable to help us for the police.

"How is André?"

"I think he is all right for now, Harry." Janine's face shining tense from the back seat. "He says it hurts, but I can see it is not bleeding much."

"Can we just get some bandages, and. . . ."

"Harry, here comes a cop." Langevin looking over his shoulder. "We're parked wrong, you must go, get out of Montreal."

Lift it into gear and slide away. Oh Jesus don't stop us officer. Just stay behind there not whistling as you slide into the rear view mirror not watching us but walking down the curb. Keep going away from here.

"He's getting cold, Harry. Can we have some heat?"

And close the windows on this warm night and on with the heater. Now Shirley watching me.

"What will you do?"

"I'm taking us to Toronto."

"Toronto! "

"Janine, get me onto the Boulevard Metropolitain." And explain as we go.

The Drive

"We can be there in a few hours. If he is all right, we
will go straight through. If not, we stop at a hospital on the way. Cornwall, Belleville. They'll never
think of looking for us in Ontario. If we have to stop, we'll
say he had a hunting accident. André can be French from
Cornwall. We can go to mother's at Port Faith. Or stay with
Magee in Toronto. André?"

"He's getting sleepy, Harry."

"Take his pulse." Now on the greenlit Metropolitan driving
west.

"We can easily hide in Toronto. It's perfect. No one will
suspect us hiding there. I know my way around there, and I
know we will be all right."

But Janine doesn't like it. "It's so far, Harry."

"I can drive it in five hours in this car. The highway is four
lanes all the way."

Silence for assent from them all. Fine to be in command.
Best solution and carry it out to save poor André.

On the coloured map of an American gas company, Canada
drawn. Free in a hundred bad colours the lines of our knowing

and going. Since I was last here, the great road completed east to west along the bottom of our country like a rule under the north. To simply turn north out of this, and anywhere along this black line, north to the lakes, the woods, the rockfires and swimming, the fish in the pan and the floating haze over the morning lake. The loons skating over the flat water swimming down and up and laughing, playing tag and laughing like children. Camp on a wet morning and the smell of the cedar path in the rain and the slippery wet hand along the rail smooth with a thousand hands against the edge of the rock falling into the black gold water.

"I don't like this. I don't want to go to Toronto."

André's blood looking for a doctor. Now Janine sounding worried.

"Harry, should we stop?"

"Trouble?"

"He is bleeding a little."

Enormous André buckled into the rear seat legs jackknifed, sleeping facedown over Janine, never complaining.

"Close the window, would you. It's cold on his face."

"I'm all right. Keep on driving." André's voice is very light.

One hand on top of our destiny at seventy-five while the other winds up the glass.

"The shirt has slipped. He'll bleed to death."

"Shut up Janine." My voice so hard. "Shirley, take his pulse."

Janine in the mirror cringing. My eyes upon her. The car a wind cave of our thoughts.

"I have no watch, Harry." Her eyes on Janine and then on André.

No watch on this violent bunch living on the edge of time.

"All right I shall hold it at sixty and tell you when one mile has passed. How do you feel André?"

"It hurts."

"Are you cold?"

"A little."

Glance again at Janine afraid in the mirror. Her slit dark

eyes now underscored with strain like a hockey player. The cold nights on the bike arriving at the arena with the fear in my guts and the terror of rising to face it alone in my room refusing not to go. Alone the cold shredded wheat in the big kitchen with the faint gas smell from the stove all night burning in the closed air. Smell of fear. Eyes on Shirley now. What is she trying to tell me? He feels cold. The car is warm.

"Shall I put the heater on high?"

"It will make you sleepy. Give him your jacket." And again one-handed at eighty left arm carefully out and her taking the other. She has seen my eyes on Janine. She knows. She knows what the tone of my voice meant just then. Shut up, woman. The male who has possessed. But that's absurd. My fear of being found out's being found out.

"Tell me when a minute has gone by." Unstiffen my right foot from this light-ended little car. God it's fast. At sixty with my eyes down from the last part of the sunset steadily holding. Not up or down a mile an hour watching the black and white tenths roll up. Shirley turned and André's eyes unexpressing.

"Eight-tenths. Nine-tenths. And now . . . one minute."

"Sixty-eight. Now do it again."

Through the night with the great moon coming up and blistering the riversea to our left occasionally hoodwinked by islands. What the hell does sixty-eight mean anyway? We don't know.

"Take my pulse, Shirl," whispering under the airstream. Do they design these cars to keep down the windnoise so you can think? The miles roll up black and white and we eternally pass the right-hand cars unpassed ourselves. Highway patrolled by aircraft it said back there. My god, caught, we are doomed with the bloodstained André. Better slow down. But okay from this steady sixty. That may have saved our lives.

"Does anyone know if we are in Ontario yet?"

Nobody answers. Are we all dead. If we are, then the plates and this car will give us away like Banquo's blood. I must get off this road and steal another . . . plates. That's it. Just steal plates.

"We have to turn off."

"Why?" from André suddenly suspicious. God how fast he suspects me now. Does he think I betrayed him? Did I?

"To get new plates. These ones will be recognized in Ontario."

"Province is full of Quebec cars. Keep going."

"Not four escaping rioters in a hot Mustang." Why did I say rioters and not that more convenient word?

"Keep going." The strange authority of his voice. But weak. Not to anger him. "Okay André."

"They get frozen on, can't get them off."

He's quite right. Shame of him being right less a gallon of blood and me not.

Green glow of the dashlight on our two front faces. When was I last in Toronto? After school, seeing Mike. In that coach-house he had behind his father's place. Where they kicked him out because he was so hard to handle. Expelled from some snooty school, I believe. Upper Canada? Someplace. And suddenly the family broke and Mike on the world alone trying to make out in Knightsbridge with me. He pawned something. That was it, at school he took a record player and pawned it. Why they kicked him out of boarding school. Always borrowing from André and me in London those days. But God, how he could blow that imaginary bugle. Swear he had one in the room and drunk with his Irishness playing a sleepy Mexican with a sombrero against the wall in the sun talking through his daze. And always to the races with your borrowed quid. Never good enough for Mike to punt without the thrill and dazzle of being at the track. But a high old time. I wonder how much he owes me at all at all.

"Harry?"

"Yes." Shirley sounds tired.

"How much longer?"

"Few hours."

"Hours?"

"Yes." Shirley glancing back at Janine and André. Both asleep. Janine faking to see what she can discover? Honest André, I did not mean anything by it. You said she had left you.

"I wondered if we should stop for something."

"More important to hurry isn't it?" Back up near ninety again. Too easy in this car.

"Perhaps. In a while, perhaps we had better stop to look to his bandages."

And she all alone sinking comfortably back into the seat not at all aware of what this is. Poor smooth child, anyway, not used to these tremendous North American distances. As Mike says, a tit-toss from Montreal to Toronto, but half a continent to them. She probably thinks we are nearly to the Pacific. Drowsing in this warm car I must talk.

"How close do you think we are to the Pacific, Shirl?"

"Pacific?"

"What's that?" She doesn't like my mimicking. "An ocean, Shirl."

"Yes, I know."

"I love you."

"About a thousand miles? Eight hundred?"

"About three thousand, five hundred. It's still afternoon there."

"Goodness."

"Excuse me for chattering, but I'm feeling sleepy. I have to stay awake in this damned little thing. It drives beautifully except it is light in the stern."

"Even with them in it?"

"Yes. Are they awake?"

"I think not."

More of the dark silence rushing past us. Bugs on the windshield. Season of fireflies past or I could show them Shirl. Telling her about them now and nights at camp when we sang lying under the tall pines and the bugle had sounded that eerie call across the flat lake and rebounding from the stone hills. Now she sleeps and the miles tire by.

Radio. Chrome switch carefully under the outreaching soft hood and do not let the car swerve as you reach. Huge and beautifully designed highway joining two incomprehensions. Comes on instantly.

. . . have been taken to hospital in critical condition. Montreal police said that various groups of Separatists were identified in the crowd, and that many people have been questioned since the explosion. Several arrests were made. Among the groups identified were members of the MSA, *the* FLQ, *and some small groups. The well-known Montreal wrestler, Jacques Beausoleil, was among those questioned by police. His wife told* CBC *reporter Tom Alpert tonight that she was sure her husband was not involved.*

"Mrs. Beausoleil do you believe your husband was implicated in this attack?"

"I do not believe. He was a member of the MSA, *true, but he did not believe to violence. To this kind of violence."*

"You imply he did believe in some kind of violence."

"Well, of course, he was a wrestler, you know. So he believed in that. But he did not believe killing. This is a terrible thing for Canada."

Montreal police could not confirm reports that members of the famous Van Doos regiment had been flown here from Churchill, Manitoba, where they had been stationed on arctic summer exercises, but an officer in the Canadian Army Headquarters in Ottawa confirmed that the report was true. Reports of further violence in Quebec have been . . . here is a report just handed to me. Police in Quebec City said tonight that a band of young students has begun a demonstration in the centre of the city. Police cars have been despatched to the area. There are no details at the moment. Reports of further demonstrations

*and violence have come to our studios from three
other centres in Quebec: Trois Rivières, Sherbrooke
and Montreal round Pie Neuf. Further despatches will
be read as they are received. The Acting Prime Minister, The Honourable Jean Desrosiers will speak to the
nation in one-half hour from now. Here are the main
items again. The Prime Minister of Canada and the
leader of the Liberal Party, the Right Honourable. . . .*

Don't let it be true.

*. . . Evan des Lauriers Price, 46, was killed tonight in
a bomb explosion in an auditorium in Montreal
where he was speaking at a Liberal Party rally. Several members of the Cabinet with him are in hospital
in Montreal. At least one bystander was believed to
have been killed. Police have questioned several hundred people and sealed off the auditorium. The acting
Prime Minister, Jean Desrosiers, has appealed to the
nation to be calm, and for residents of Quebec to
co-operate with police. We return you now to our
studios in Ottawa.*

Music, music from an organ. Another station. No one awake?
All sleeping through riot and storm. To wake André. Pile
through the night alone, there is nothing else to do.

But quietly to another station. Static and interference. Slow
down and try to tune. Cops all over this highway now. Bomb,
André. Did you know? Was it your cell?

Impossible to be silent. Pointless to wake him now. Where
the hell are we? Shall I turn off and give us up while all sleep?
Cross the median the moment I see a cop coming? Couple
more hours to Toronto, dump him in hospital and run and
hide? How did I get into this mess anyway? Price, Evan something or other Price, killed. His picture in all the papers. The
young scion from a fine old family . . . somewhere around
here? Belleville? Brockville? No, in that little tit of land half-

French, half-English near the border where the Ottawa goes to the St. Lawrence. God, he wasn't much over forty-five it seemed. Wiped out by a bomb. In quiet Canada. But it wasn't that loud. I remember it, just a smoke bomb. Try another station.

Swivel the knob around, find something. All these cars lit up at night tunnelling through the blackness with the radio on listening to death and all among it.

Breathless announcer this time with something about the hospital. Can't get news. Shouting in the background. Reporter on the street in Montreal now.

A huge crowd has gathered outside the Montreal General Hospital. It is impressively quiet here just now. There must be nearly ten thousand people in the grounds of the hospital keeping vigil for the injured inside. I have seen several priests walking among the crowd and in at least one case, a priest supporting a woman in tears.

"What is it Harry? What are you listening to?"
"Shirley, the Prime Minister was killed in that explosion."
"Are you sure?"
"That's what the radio said."

. . . hundred policemen watching the crowd, but they are not necessary. This appears to be a spontaneous demonstration from the hearts of the people. Rumours are circulating in this crowd that the Prime Minister has been revived by open-heart massage but this is not confirmed, and appears to be wishful thinking. The latest report from the doctors in the hospital is the same one we had two hours ago, that the Prime Minister suffered severe internal injuries and probably head injuries from the bomb and the fall from the plat-

form, and that his heart stopped beating in the ambu-
lance carrying him here. There has been no further
word except to say that none of the Cabinet members
appears to have been seriously hurt. I'll now return
you to our studios while I go nearer the main door of
the hospital and try to interview some of this very
mixed crowd speaking several languages as they keep
their vigil on this night of tragedy for the nation.
Wait a minute, something is happening here, some
people are gathering, and a noise . . . excuse me, may I
get through . . . singing. Or . . . they appear to be pray-
ing. People are kneeling here, ladies and gentlemen,
they appear to be saying a prayer in unison. This is a
moment of great reverence and emotion in the sloping
grounds of this great hospital as these masses of
people kneel spontaneously to offer a prayer . . . I
think you can hear the massed voices of the people in
many tongues. . . .

Mumble through the radio mixed with the tire whine and
windrace. Volume down.

"Hadn't we better wake André?"

"What can he do now? I better keep driving."

"Janine? Did you hear the news?"

"Yes, I was listening."

"Are you sure André is all right?"

"He is breathing. He is just asleep. I can see the shirt and
there is no fresh blood."

"I think we had better turn off and go to the hospital."

"No. Not yet. Toronto."

Sound of Janine weeping. Oh, this forsaken country mur-
dering, bombing, destroying.

Green signs going by on a highway they have pulled out of
the earth with their monstrous claws since I left. Been at St.
Zotique. Gananoque. Thousand Islands. Bridge to the U.S.A.
YIELD, Ontario. No left merge. The graceful bridge lifted over
the river reflecting its lights. Why a symbol of hopelessness to

me, that water dark below shinily uselessly reflecting the beautiful lights above. Hopeless, hopeless love of the dark river for the tall lights in its heart. Kingston so many miles, and Port Faith in that sign ahead. Where? The hospital there for André. Too significant. Too obvious. Known in a moment. But I would be free of him at last. To cast him off now that he has done this murder into the bright lights where he will be saved to hang on an Ontario gibbet. Swing over the dark river and die with your boots in it killer Frenchman. Janine in tears blowing her nose. Free of it and out at last to do what I need away from this country's madness. Take King Street to Port Faith and let the law deal with its own Harry where you are known. Where the people call you their own after so many years and you are still among them. Just a little hard right at that green-edged boulevard coming up to the right leading into it. Port Faith one street now on the passing highway littered with our bones and coffee cups. This would be all over with one hard right switch of the wheel into a concrete abutment. Like this one coming up. Stately passing with tremendous speed. Another up there coming to us. Just a quick wrench right into it and all translated into the next dimension so close now, so near and ready for us hungering for us having just taken in Price. Back there lies our image of death the wrecked car smoking wheels turning still in the air and we all dead in its frozen wreck. They don't know sitting beside me I want to flip right and kill us all. And do it Harry do it. Nonono screaming and tearing within me. So close and easy to do, moment wrench and gone gone gone. No right. No right over death. Leans close in the car and whispers to me and no one hears it. Must stop. I am going to do it. Must stop and rest. Slowing stopping and at last doing the little right wrench at tiny miles per hour safely onto the margin.

"Harry?"

"Gotta stop." Panting. Weak. Hang head over wheel. Get out. Long door swinging to admit me to the night and out.

"Are you all right?"

"No."

171

"What's the matter?"

Oh what to say? We are driving a killer. Stopped car shakes to wham of the trucks' pass. Out. No sickness now. A clear head. Walk around the front. I took the keys. Crushed in my hand hurting. Down the bank. Up to the fence. Chirping sounds. Grass. Pricking. No knees to pray on. But lie on the August hard earth and let it come. The killing words. It is my clear responsibility to him and to me to do it. Take him there and believe what he said.

"Is there anything I can do?" Sound of her grasssteps coming and me beginning to feel stagey lying here now that it has somewhat passed. The speed of revelation. The lightning pause of knowing. Hah. Another phony word-game within me converting instantly to lightflash on canvas, knowing how to do it and trying to remember the moment as it disappears knowing it can't be remembered, and able above me lying to speak back at her simplest words "No. I will" far away speaking "be all right in a minute. Just lie here with me," and even aware now thinking of him, bleeding in the car sinking beside me uncareful for her English dress. "Just tired, that's all."

And only sitting beside a hand on my head coolly.

"Shirley, it's so terrible. That man is dead. What is our responsibility?" She does not know and carefully does not say. I must recover myself. I have lived such a bad life, such a stupid life and here it is proved lying stranded on the grass faced with either of two betrayals my country my friend having already betrayed myself and Shirley. Opened wounds into myself and others. Living badly, living the worst of lives stupidly bouncing from one catastrophe I did not know I was committing to another. What is my next one. Committing even now. The ignorance of evil. And all a stupid person can do is remember and make no vows.

"Can you still drive?"

"Yes."

"Come on then." Now standing and holding out her hand to me. That's twice for you Shirl, and when do I start?

"Okay, I'll be all right."

But still waiting. What does she think, what does somebody else outside me think. Am I going crazy in here alone?

"Shirley, what should I do?"

"I don't know Harry. I just don't know."

"I think I should believe him. I think I should get him to a hospital."

"Oh yes. Of course."

"What do you mean, then, you don't know?"

"I'm sorry. I wasn't sure what you meant. The news is so awful, I thought you meant something else, and I feel so sad about it, about André."

"Let's go. I didn't mean to get after you."

Back to the car again and keep on driving. No more radio news but just get to Mike's place. Hide and be safe. One bit at a time.

⁂

Feared Toronto on the horizon suddenly. My metropolitan hatred. On this slanting downward hillside towards the night-time west, towers bluntly rising from the far grass. The new light on them. Stop to stare over the sleeping hillside of houses and green lawns scarcely awakening into the built promise of the city.

"We're here."

André widely awake now looking about us. Presumably all the English signs hitting his eyes rudely. How suddenly I want to speak French back at him and remove the fixation. We're really all right, you know, André, we really are. City which I have never imagined, unimaginable Toronto, give us a home. Don't betray us. And along smooth highways with our shadow running widely ahead of us trying to catch the next breath of road jittering in the speed. Fender mirror bloated with the gold bright sun behind. It will have to be Michael in this city where we are at last not known.

the
lonely
ones

Toronto

"Harry, we're hungry." How Shirley addresses me
now on their behalf. The frightened eyes of Janine
upon us. Acting on their behalf. Yes.

"Okay. I know a place on Yonge we can stop."

But Yonge may elude me on this fantastic stretch of ever-
widening highway. Like a tarmac with all the plane cars guided
in the white lines never slowing. Signs. Interchange. I'd better
slow. Where are we with all these early-morning trucks bombing by and the splits and curves and turns I don't know unable
to left or right from these expanding lanes. What kind of a
city is this anyway. Welcomes you in and speeds you on in the
same sign. Take off to Windsor via Yonge Street to City Hall
next left yield 400 north 4¾ miles feeder lane. And it's all
French to them.

Well here's for a right and watch that farm truck. Paved
shoulder at sixty. Just hug it boy and garrot this damn wheel
next chance you get.

"I'm sweating. May I open a window, André?"

"Yes."

What did Mike call it? Santa Claus something. Yes. Bel-
gravian Embassy? The Santa Claus. Yes. St. Nicholas Street.
That's where. Directions from gas station attendant waiting

in this horrible gaslight of morning surrounded by rush-hour buggies chuffing downtown. Things will be better. Pay him out of the money belt and silently join the great belch lurching south in the monster city. All the pretty people waiting in summer dresses at their buses staidly to go downtown and do it while we revolve our revolution on four wheels to Mike's place.

Finally this alley away from sunlight and park outside this dusty cardboard sign on red bricks or cobbles to knock at Mike.

"I'll be back in a second. You'd better wait here." Up these stairs and be up Mike for once in your life. A blast of the puckerlips trumpet. Knock. Sounds within. Mike. Slippering over and his face wide-eyed at the door opening to admit.

"Michael. How are you this sweltering morning?"

"Fine. Yourself?"

"What's the matter?"

"What time is it?" And him in pyjamas.

"I don't know. Late, I guess. Mike, I wouldn't come unheralded if it were not an emergency. Can I step in and explain?"

Closing the door behind him as he steps out. Red-striped pyjamas and evil early breath from endless revels.

"What's the problem, Harry?"

"Look, old cod, it's great to see you. I'm sorry to arrive this way, but I am in trouble."

"I see." Narrow and black-Irish face seaming with a touch of welcome. Now yawns. "Where did you come from? Are the police on to you?"

"Not yet. Listen, I have people waiting in the car. Can I bring them up?"

"Well, sure. Maybe. And what is the problem?"

"Is this your pad?"

"Sort of a nightclub I started. Warehouse, actually. I have part of it as a flat. Have you got a cigarette?"

"No. Look, can we shelter here?"

"I guess so. Come on in."

To go in for a moment to humour him. After all, roused with a hangover.

"The problem is Mike, that, well, there are three of them waiting. Shirley too."

"Shirley? What happened?'

"Impossible to explain just now. But I brought André Riancourt with me. You remember him and his wife, Janine."

"Yes?"

"We were hung up in Montreal last night at a political rally. André was at this meeting where the bomb went off. He was injured, he belongs to some Separatist group, supposed to raid a radio station, and he would be suspected. He couldn't go to hospital there. He needs attention. We wanted to keep him here till we could get him to a doctor. He obviously couldn't check into the Royal York. We had to have somewhere to go."

"You have been playing around. What happened to that weird society you belonged to in London. Scientologists."

"I never belonged to that. You mean that school in the west end."

"Yeah, the face-to-face personality-discovering thing. But bombs?"

"Oh that was for kicks. I mean, London. Now is different. I'll explain later. Can I bring them up?"

"Look, what do you mean about bombs? I mean this place probably isn't insured."

"Mike, it's asking a lot, but did I ever. . . ."

"Go on, last week there was some madman in here recruiting candidates to blow up the U.S. consulate and the cops came looking for him. Damn near had a riot. Turned out he was a draft dodger from the States. Was in touch with Ho Chi Minh by ouija board and this place is suspect enough already. So. . . ."

"No bombs. And no cops if we keep it absolutely quiet. My whereabouts are unknown."

"I know that bit. You remember the day. . . ."

"Be right up."

And clatter downstairs. Help André up the stairs easily now. Keep my arm low for the shirt on his back. Just crusty with dark blood higher up and his eyes half closed.

"You okay, André?"

"Tired. It hurts a bit. Not bad." Just help him past Mike's surprise at the door and to the bed. Vasty hall full of tables stretching in after-smoke darkness away in dim light as we take André quietly to the screened-off part where Mike's warmth and shape are still on the bed. Face down and flat so his head is comfortable. How quietly we introduce Janine and Mike. And he is courtly with Shirley and we play out this disorder. A phone and to call the hospital. Not far away.

"Let Janine and Shirley take him, do you think?"

Mike standing back observing. Now having changed from the washroom over there. Janine questioning why the girls should take him.

"Much less suspicious, I think. Janine, you're his wife, you see, and Shirley, the next door neighbour. You drove him down."

"I thought you said we would tell them it was a hunting accident."

"Well, that won't work. I've been thinking. They'll suspect something. Hunting where? At this time of year?"

"I don't think I need to go." André half asleep on the bed.

"André, let me just have a look. I'll be careful." And Shirley and Janine at last in decent light can gently lift the shirt just to where it won't pull off blood clots. Just gently. André lying quiet as we murmur over him. Long bad gash. White. Bone, muscles, gristle. Can't leave it.

"Look, we'll say he fell downstairs and cut himself on a bottle. Nobody heard him; it was last night; he lay there. That accounts for how it is dried. But we can't leave it. It's too dangerous. Infection. God, André, this could be bad if you leave it."

"I can't move my right arm properly."

"You've got to get somebody to stitch you up. I don't care if it isn't bleeding much. We've got to try this."

"What do we say for an address, and the rest? They ask a lot of questions in hospital."

"Well, then he was working here, it happened here. And he is visiting from Sudbury, or somewhere. Give a fake address there. They won't check."

"They might. What if they do?" And all look at me as if I am responsible.

"Then it's a chance. We have to take it. Damnit, we can't leave it like this. All right, I'll go too."

"I'll go." Mike surprisingly volunteering. "You need a rest, Harry, you looked bushed. Besides I've got the Ontario Hospital Insurance card, and we can get André in on that. He won't have to say anything much, and he can kind of slur his words, besides, he's sick and they won't suspect anything. If they ask about his accent – and why should they – he can say it was Mikolaisjch and he changed it when he came to Canada.

"Yeah. That would be great. Would you do that Mike?"

"Sure. Let's go." And as simply as that, they go downstairs with the Mustang keys in Mike's hands, and off to the good old Toronto hospital to make it fine again.

And such a big hurdle is so easily passed. André will be fine, and we'll plan from there. Spend tonight here.

What did this use to be? Huge old warehouse or something, Mike said. They'll be a couple of hours. But what if they want to have André in for a night of observation? That'll be okay. He can just stay. But all he has to do is get that thing stitched up and he'll be fine. We disinfected it with that stuff we got in St. Zotique, and it doesn't look too bad this morning. I'm sure he'll be all right. And as I come back to this spot in the downtown blue of this place, I realize I have paced the entire perimeter of this nightclub of Mike's and noticed almost nothing. Good thing I don't have to dress anything for another TV show. But Jesus to get back to our painting and forget for a while.

To lie down on Mike's sofa here hands behind head and

dream of something. Just close my eyes and dream of a couple of days up north fishing. Float out on the lake in a canoe in the morning and watch the mist balloon up as the sun just gets above the trees. That first morning out, waking up suddenly in the tent and you look up at the canvas, and you realize that it is getting a little lighter, and suddenly you've got to get up. Only a couple of the birds singing, and everything wet, and now wind, and you hear maybe a rapids far away that you can't hear any other time of day running in the woods where you paddled down yesterday and saw the moose running with the big jumpy look up out of the shallows and back into the woods where you will never see him again. Into the dark woods, all so quiet and peaceful and still and undisturbed, and you are in it all alone, beautiful and taking the canoe down the river just where you want to go. A hummingbird at the portage midsummer day. Loon in the quiet light in the dawn overhead, and the sound of its wings very gentle like a drummer with the wires just brushing dreamily at the end of the night. In this quiet place.

Noises up the stair. André coming in at the door standing upright. Looking big and mean.

"Hey, how are you man? Was it okay?"

"It was fine. Now let's go."

"Go? Go where?"

"Montreal."

"Montreal. What the hell. We just got here." The girls looking sheepish. Something has been happening.

"Where's Mike?" And nobody answers. "Where is Mike?"

"Harry, he left." Shirley looking white with worry.

Getting up fast and running down the room at them. "What happened?"

"I had a fight with your Mr. Magee."

"A fight? What do you mean? Did he hurt you?"

André going down the room away from me. What is the

matter with him. The pair of them against the pair of us. This is fantastic. "Look, André, what happened?"

"Nothing serious. I argued with your Mr. Magee and he got out of the car, that's all."

"What the hell were you arguing about?"

"He blamed our group for killing Evan Price, and I said we had nothing to do with it, that it was a group that we were not associated with. He said that we were all responsible for having made such a noise, and I told him he was stupid."

"You told him he was a dumb Irishman." And Janine drawing her lips down with that inhibited smile. "So he left."

"I see. Well, don't worry, he's just a dumb Irishman, he'll get over it."

But the joke doesn't get near André who continues standing there.

"What did the doctors say?"

"Go home and get some rest."

"I've been thinking, we could go up north to this cottage I know about. Wait till things cool down a bit."

"We have to go back right away." André accenting the last, and walking round the far end of the room. To advance towards him in this cavernous silence is somehow menacing. What is the matter with him.

"You need some rest, André. We shouldn't go back right away. We can just take a couple of days at the cottage."

"I won't go." André saying this straight at me. Like an accusation.

"Why not?"

"You know. You know, Harry." And walks down the room with only Janine beside him talking low. What the hell is the matter with him all of a sudden. What does he know? Is it Janine and me? Is it that finally?

"Harry."

"Yes, Shirley." Not able really to look at her.

"Sit down, Harry." And her words, her tone, inevitably Shirley come in and undo me. Collapsing in the chair. Watching André far down the room. "What the hell is the matter with him?" but not really feeling my puzzlement or anger. I know what is the matter with you now old man, and it is the matter with me as well, and we are all unfaithful. It is simply that we are all unfaithful. It is not even as complex as being complex, not just the having of these shifting levels, it is only that when it comes to this room now with you, I cannot deny it, I have betrayed you, and you know it whatever I say. Even if I admit it is true, you know it is truer than I can admit. And there is no admission of this, because there is no living with it, and what I have created, I cannot endure for so long. Yet you know I love you. If I could look this love down the room to you, I would do it now.

André suddenly shouting at me "Hey, Harry, why don't you call the cops now? Tell me, why don't you call the cops?" Standing at the far end of the room looking down the darkness at me shouting "Tell me."

"Why André? Why? Did you do it?" walking towards him. And André's face terrible and dark, and I see he did not do it, he did not know anyone was going to kill Price.

"What do you mean do it?"

"Was it false pretences? Did you get me in there to help kill him? Was that it?"

"No. I didn't know." And it is true and he is blushing because he is ashamed, he has been caught, they didn't trust him enough to tell him. He wasn't in on it. Phrasing the questions to fire at him and they are all useless. Because we are both guilty and all guilty.

"You don't believe me Harry. Arrest me then. Go on."

"The martyr."

"You got everything else. What do you want, to have the revolution too, is that it? Go ahead, arrest me. You took everything else. Why don't you take the revolution." And he is deliberately standing away from Janine saying he knows it all. Janine looking frozen-faced at me.

"It's not your revolution, André."

"Are you lying? Did you bring me here to give me to the cops?"

Standing back a distance from him looking down the room still as if he is about to fire at me. "I wouldn't bother."

"I know what you have been doing."

"Will you shut up?"

"Answer my question."

"Baby, I'm not taking this from you, you've given it to me. You know that."

But his eyes are shaded, I can't see into him right now standing beside Janine so stagily I can't believe it is him, full of emotion, choking him with anymoment hate. I can't say anything more André, baby, you'll have to believe me for once in your French life. You have sent this thing and it's too late to get it back.

"That's crazy Harry. You want it all, eh. What, does the Anglo get the province and the money and the resources and the women and the paintings too, and then take over the revolution. Is that it, eh?"

"Look, André, I've had enough of your shit right now, you know that, no more shit out of you while you're sick."

"Go and hit me too, and call the cops."

"Goddamn you, will you listen to me. I'm trying to tell you. . . ."

"Trying to tell me how to run my revolution against you. . . ."

"When are you going to understand that this isn't a race riot, when in hell are you going to understand that?"

"I've told you that already myself, Harry. I know that." And his face so hot isn't sick now; it is just staring at me telling me something. The same thing I'm telling him.

"And it is not over, André."

"No, it isn't over. It isn't over, it has just started, you know it has, it has just started, I see that, I'm trying to tell you that, so don't start taking it away from me Harry. I know where I'm going, I know what I'm doing, so don't start to run me, Harry. Just keep it like it was, okay? Is that okay Harry?" Shouting.

"Goddamnit, goddamn you André." Shout at the bastard

looking so smug about being wrong. "If I wanted to take over that's where I'd be right now, because I know where this thing is going and you don't seem to know any more. I know what it is just as you do, and if I didn't want you, you wouldn't be here now man, you understand that, you wouldn't BE here." And stick my face at him to let him see, and show you this, André baby, see me here, you don't know it but I am helping you if you will only goddamn let me.

"You arrogant tourist Anglo bastard, Harry, goddamn you, don't tell me what I've been doing, don't tell me who I am."

"I'm not."

"Then don't talk to me like that. Don't do that, Harry, I might kill you."

"Kill me, kill me? I'm the only thing that keeps you from turning this into a race war, and you're going to kill me and ruin the whole thing."

"Shut up Harry."

"You only wanted me like the house Jew André, isn't that it?" and walk down the room to get right up to this and see him in the face now and let it all out. "I'm just the pet Anglo to prove it was all okay for your conscience. And now it's a big deal, big threat, when I suddenly get some ideas, when I'm going to DO something, when I'm going to help you, when I already did help you. Is that it André, that you're too god-damned proud to need me?"

"No. You know that isn't true."

"Then for Christ's sake listen to me. You're alone here, you don't know anybody, the Prime Minister of this country is dead and in his grave, and you don't know enough to stay out of the way of the police until they catch the guys who did it." See him looking at me knowing I'm starting to talk sense.

"Will you take us back?"

"Yes, but later. We stay here now, and we go up north to a cabin which I know about, and we lie low there for a while until you feel better and things in Montreal simmer down, and we decide then what to do. Maybe we go out west, maybe we go up north, maybe we come back here where the action is,

183

and maybe we stay put a while longer. I don't know. We'll decide. *You'll* decide. But we don't go back to Montreal, we don't go back to Quebec, until our own sweet time."

And the girls have accepted that already, I can feel it in Janine looking at André, and the soft bewilderment in Shirley's face. And it is Shirley who unexpectedly asserts herself. "I think it would be foolish to go back to Montreal now, especially when people are so excited. The police will be forced to find someone, and you are so close to it André, that they are bound to hold you and question you. And who knows how people will react if they suspect you did it."

"I think so, André," and Janine looks the anxious lover now, pathetic in her dark-lined face and eyes concentrating on him. Why are they crowding him now when he has so obviously decided. Or did I imagine it?

"Sure, Harry, sure, all this is fine and it is all beside the point." And I can feel him now, crowding me, making me say it, making me commit myself. "Now tell me where this is all going."

"Okay, André, listen, it is going here right here into the gut, right into people where they live, finally, this country is going to wake up and, oh, it's going to make war. Yes."

"War on what?" Your big speech, Harry.

"War on the finagling crappists. Will you take that, André?" and fall over on Mike's couch laughing war on the finagling crappists indeed whoever they are know thy enemy and I think it is time to get drunk, yes indeed it is time to get drunk and there is a noise down the room far away which seems to be someone coming in, and it is Michael coming in the door with huge cartons of food and still I have not settled it with André, something has to be faced out with him, some final decision taken here and now. "What do you say André? The war on crap."

And this is what we get. Great. This is the battle cry. And his long revolutionary countenance falls into a stein of capitalist beer and looks at me with some joy written in it somewhere. It will be better. And it is definitely time now to drink and to enjoy fine peaceful Toronto with rich and prosperous Mike at the helm of this swinging ship.

"Wherewith to eat and sup," intones Michael advancing down the room with huge cartons steaming at the ready. "Pizza and lasagna to go and lots of chianti. Is anyone interested in chianti?"

"Three cheers for Michael. Hip Hip, MaGee, and Hip Hip MaGee hits the ceiling. And fade in the tearing and scratching of humans eating Italian food to go, Italian food coming and Italian food gone, in tasty cardboard boxes, all for breakfast with the good old gang in the back room of Santa Claus' Bag, good old Michael's fine old restaurant on St. Nicholas Street. Yes, it is a good day and "All hail you Michael, and your wherewith to eat and sup. May it always stand at the ready, and keep the coffin lid from closing tight" and a hoist of the plastic orange juice glass filled with fine old Niagara Malmsey to you indeed, indeed.

"Jesus, Michael, here is the very pub we often discussed in glorious days gone by, which you would run and I would advertise to all, here it is at last, in our very hands, and glad to be home with you tonight by the fire, and it cold and windy out of doors."

"Hottest goddamn night in twenty-six years, and the dom foule says it's cold and windy. It's windy inside if you ask me. Now you take your average summer night, he'll resist, but if you ask him nicely to come along there Billy, he'll go like snow off a ditch, by the jeez" and the fine old Purry Sound fairmer comes out in his eyebrows raised, lip over the gumtucked country suckerlook. And how marvellous Michael does it so well with his radio voice pitched low and fine to the microphone audience way out there in the snowy wastes beyond these city grimy windows, listening to every clever word from his broadcasting mind. How I would like to have Michael's humorous despotism. He is making this party, just making it for us walking round entertaining us. And here are some CBC types coming now too to the nightclub as it is. Help us down the keg if I leave any for us near the grapeskinned bottom.

"Mike, I've got plenty of green" standing near him a little away from the others so they don't hear me conspiring to help for this night's revelry. It can only be late afternoon, and yet near Michael it seems always night and party time.

"A couple of my friends from the CBC are going to drop over after their show later on," says Michael. "Do you want to be on television, maybe with the action painting bit. You could always get some chick to cover herself with red ochre number six or something like that and paint her with your very own brush."

"That stuff is poisonous. I wouldn't ask any girl I liked to do a thing like that. I'd rather do her myself, there Billy," and draw the lips charmingly down and dumbgaze at Michael. While André stands and stares smiling at the gaze but perhaps not realizing that this is our Beauce farmer, our Ban weh, our very own mire and pire of the family farm from Purry Sound to Burry with a squerl in a burrl. "And there you are, Billy," with the paper cup now topped up. "Fine old Niagara Whimsy, there, Michael. Aged in the truck on the way over, I'll wager."

"You're right, there, and what was all that about paying me for it."

"Listen, I guess you must owe me about six hundred gallons of this moosepiss, eh, man, after that marvellous Morgan that you drove and never paid one ounce of gas for? Or am I exaggerating your defalcations once again, to quote from your balmy days?"

Michael standing tall and looking round. What a tall gathering it is near each other in this vasty hall, tall André with the beard looking solemnly owlish at us at last a little reconciled to our Torontoness, and Shirley pale and fresh as water after all this night and day, and Janine still nervous and dark and looking intensely around for the treachery that dwells in her own dark soul. Or is it mine, and only she can mine it. But Michael is calling someone through this wine haze that with the heat and fear and driving all night has got me reeling about till I hear police cells and sirens in the distance of this huge thundering town. Oh yes, no longer the magnolias and fresh maple leaves of spring I remember in this amazing city. Michael slit green eyes peering round us. Both he and André, yet his are yellow-green, devil-green, liffey-green, and André's are sea-green, blue-green, skypeering-green of good paint. Standing in our quartet plus one here now surrounded by the crowd of CBC types and listening to Michael rave about the old days there and why it was great in London when the fifties were still on and they weren't dead yet as they are now bankrupt. So it is us now, if Michael is right, only us, for even the Americans have fucked it up and thrown it away and we are the only people left in the west who have a chance and we can't kick it away, it is too important and standing here listening to you Michael, looking down into our glasses as we all solemnly do who have drunk a bit too much. Yes, and the television chappies are here now with their cameras mounted on a curiously old-fashioned-looking brown wooden tripod with the lights aside it and the man next it very yellow in the face, obviously a jaundiced man, with wide ears which he now slaps into the huge brown plastic muffs and starts to record all this for a waiting posterity.

"Michael, and I've just made a fine phrase to write home to your old mither in Purry Sound. Do you see the lads over there waiting to record all this for posterity?" And saying it, realizing it, what it is for, not posterity but something else, for people to watch soon, on a program which might be watched by cops. And there is Shirley over there. Must get to Shirley through this huge crowd, Shirley talking to men who are looking down at her first and gazing round the room looking for other girls to look at. This is incredible. We are in public and we have not realized it. "Shirley, I must talk to you." Pull her away.

"How drunk do you think I am?"

"Not drunk. Your voice is a bit slow."

"Do you realize what is happening here? We are being filmed. Michael is having this whole thing filmed right now

and those are gun mikes over there, and this is all for television. For his show."

"It can't be." And looking with her at the guy with the gun
mike on stage aimed at André. And the guy with the old
camera mounted on a wooden tripod looking around for another shot, and the brown huge plastic earmuffs over his head
bent and staring, yellow-brown and intent in his blue flannel
shirt. The man beside him talking. Jesus, this is incredible,
only Michael knew.

"We mustn't make a fuss, Harry. Don't move." Shirley intently holding onto me looking around. "I'll go over and talk
to André and warn him. You go see Mike." Shirley having
amazingly taken over strikes through the crowd like a good
revolutionary and here we are, Michael me lad.

"Michael, what the hell is this? Who are these film people
and why are they here?"

"Harry, I'd like you to meet George Davidson. From one of
our senior agencies here in town."

A huge blandy man looking over me with his large blond
hand out while I nail Mike. "I asked you, Mike, what the hell
is this?"

"Just some background shots."

"You don't waste holy mother corporation's film like this
on nothing. What is it, dammit?"

"Harry, please, it's just some routine background party
shooting for a film. We need some background footage, that's
all. Don't be so immodest." And looking with his old liar's
face down at me.

"You fucking treacherous liar. It's for your show.
Separatists caught. PM's assassins nailed on TV show. These
guys are shooting us and I know it, they have the gun mikes on
us right now."

"Harry, really, your language, this whole party was set up
ages ago, and all this was arranged. Maybe the cameramen
like your face."

"Michael, I ought to slug you. This is – oh hell –" and wind
up and let you have it right into the gut and the large blond

man standing back politely and staring at me and the hand-held film man closing in and now with the huge kick to his camera and seize it and out the window and turn and there is André staring at me. Reach down to prostrate Mike and take the Mustang keys. Nobody touches me. Too amazed.

"André, get out, get out, they're filming us, out" and Shirley running through the stunned crowd standing staring at me smoking and holding their glasses and staring at me frozen in a time clip, all your waistcoats and blond hairwigged people, and you cigarette smokers and talkers who do not speak running down the stairs to the car with your blondly smoothed hair back looking down your tall noses at me and mine goodbye to your psychedelic waistcoats and your jingling drinks and your strapped and pointed bosoms and the flare of your hood ornaments in the pale daylight, the talk you have left behind you lost in the clipped broadloom where you have not lived with your growing and middle-aged sag hanging over your belly bands like the smile of the apeminded, you who have not understood wherever you were in the room talking and not hearing, goodbye, hey goodbye, you didn't know, hey watch it we're going, you didn't understand, and we are gone, yes we are gone down the stairs and out the door Janine and Shirley running, the mad Frenchman and me.

Down the stairs and out both mad from trying to stay sane in this country, but we'll make it. We made it this far and this isn't the end, oh no, you haven't won with the cops politics bombs ancestors hate, no, you lose you've been losing all the time and that's why we aren't bitter, go, go.

"How are you? How's the back? Come on." Running. The car.

"OK. I'll make it."

"Yeah, come on, we'll make it."